E-mail from: Mit
Turning Point, Te
To: Dan Egan, fire

I felt it in my bones
Hurricane Damon
last message I can get to you until this demon storm blows through. We're looking for a hit sometime around midnight.

Amy Sherwood, the doctor you sent down to help us, is worth her weight in gold. She's been out on rescues with Sheriff Jesse Boone, and I'm hoping she'll be back to deal with any injuries in case those damn meteorologists are right and this hurricane is as powerful as they've predicted.

Trouble is, I don't know where Amy is right now. Turns out she and Jesse set off to find Jesse's nephew. He and his fool teenage friends headed down to surf the giant waves in the Gulf.

The lights are flickering now, and the wind is so loud I can't hear myself think. Damon is only a few miles away. I may have lost contact with the brave emergency personnel you sent to help us—Nate, Dana, Cheryl and Amy—but I know as sure as my name is Mitch Kannon that they're all okay. Trust me on this, Dan. And as soon as the storm is over, I'll track them down, and you'll be the first to know they're safe.

Darlene Scalera, a native New Yorker, graduated magna cum laude from Syracuse University with a degree in public communications. Darlene lives happily ever after in upstate New York with her husband and their two teenage children.

Visit her at www.darlenescalera.com.

HARD RAIN

DARLENE
SCALERA

All the characters in this book have no existence outside the imagination of the author, and have no relation whatsoever to anyone bearing the same name or names. They are not even distantly inspired by any individual known or unknown to the author, and all the incidents are pure invention.

First published in Great Britain 2005
Silhouette Books, Eton House, 18-24 Paradise Road, Richmond, Surrey TW9 1SR

Darlene Scalera is acknowledged as the author of this work.

ISBN 0 373 61299 0

156-0405

Printed and bound in Spain
by Litografia Rosés S.A., Barcelona

Dear Reader,

Not all angels have wings. We call them doctors, nurses, firefighters, EMTs, officers of the law—people who day in and day out serve and safeguard society. Some have devoted their professional lives; others volunteer their personal time. Many of you reading this now are members of these selfless ranks. You are the inspiration behind the CODE RED series.

I was honoured to work with so many talented authors and editors to bring you these stories of angels on earth. In *Hard Rain*, a dedicated single-mum doctor and a courageous small-town sheriff battle not only disaster but also their own hearts as they face their greatest professional and personal challenges. I hope you enjoy their journey as they learn that some forces of nature can't be fought.

I'd love to hear from you. Simply log on to my website at www.darlenescalera.com to leave me an e-mail, check out my news, enjoy an excerpt from my latest release or get a sneak preview of what's coming up.

All my best,

Darlene

CHAPTER ONE

THE DAY began gray and cloudy. The birds still sang. The grasslands bowed to the breeze. Seven hundred National Guard troops had been put on alert by the end of yesterday. The governor had already proclaimed a state of emergency.

Sheriff Jesse Boone turned onto a side road, then another, avoiding the main road through Turning Point.

Bulletin. Advisory Number Eighteen. National Weather Service Miami Florida… The center of the tropical storm was located near latitude 27.4 north…longitude 98.1 west.

Coastal and low-country residents had begun evacuating yesterday. The interstate was bumper to bumper. Forty miles inland, Turning Point was part of the evacuation route. In twenty-four hours, the town's population had swelled.

The system is moving toward the northeast near six miles per hour…nine kilometers per hour…

The storm was crossing the Gulf leisurely, gathering strength.

> Tropical-storm-force winds extend outward up to 115 miles from the center…maximum wind speeds reaching 125 miles per hour.

The fury was small but ferocious. Its name was Damon.

The voice of Fire Chief Mitch Kannon came over the radio, cutting short the advisory. Like the majority of Turning Point's emergency services, Mitch was a volunteer.

"Dan's crew from California got here. Flew into Corpus Christi around dawn. Damn lucky. Last commercial flight to come in. Others are being cancelled or rerouted because of the watch."

Doc Holland, the town's only doctor, had suffered a heart attack and was recovering in a Houston hospital. The fire department's one paid EMT had recently married and moved to North Dakota. Even before the hurricane warning was issued, Turning Point's emergency services had been stretched thin. When the hurricane watch became a warning and coastal residents began heading inland, Mitch had contacted Dan Egan. Dan was fire chief in Courage Bay, a small coastal city in southern California, but he'd been born and raised in Turning Point.

"Took us a while to get here from Christi with all the traffic," Mitch grumbled. "I hadn't even finished briefing them before the calls started coming in. Lily Browning went into labor. Never fails when the pressure drops. Of course, Gabe's out of town. Jolene had just come in and was manning the radio until Ruth got here. Minute she heard the news about her neighbor she jumped on the call. I made her take the paramedic that came in from California with her up to the Rock-a-Bye Ranch."

Jesse half smiled as he scanned the road. "Not without a fight I'll bet." Jolene was Mitch's daughter and as headstrong as she was fearless and loyal.

"She was none too happy about it. Afraid the poor paramedic—Nate Kellison—will bear the brunt of it, but Jolene's along five months herself now. I don't like the idea of sending anyone out on a call alone if I can help it, and especially my pregnant daughter. But with all these people coming into town, the calls are starting to follow."

"Don't you worry about Jolene. She can take care of herself." As she'd proved to everyone in Turning Point after the tragic death of her husband almost five months before—only days before she learned about her own pregnancy. "So, everyone's out on calls already?"

"The team's EMT just left to fly up with Micky Flynn in the turboprop to pick up those scouts and their leader. But there's a trauma nurse and an ER resident getting ready to start setting up a triage area."

"I'm on my way to check out things at the high school. It's filling up pretty quickly. If a member of the team is available, I'd like one of them to come with me to assess the setup, look over the school nurse's station and suggest any other supplies or equipment that should be brought in."

"You bring another nurse into Flo's territory, she's going to get huffy."

Jesse smiled. The school nurse, Florence Templeton, was two years from retirement and had spent a lifetime soothing students and defusing catastrophes. She did not take kindly to outside interference.

"Maybe not if it's a doctor," Jesse suggested. "How about I swing by the station after I check in at my office, pick up the doctor and bring him over to lend a hand?"

As Jesse spoke, a broken tree limb spun crazily across the road. He turned the wheel, swerving to avoid the branch. It moved on into a field. The wind was picking up. The temperature was dropping. Jesse could feel it in his bones.

"It's a—" Static crackled over the line, cutting short the chief, as the rising wind played with the communication waves.

"What'd you say?" Jesse asked the chief once the channel cleared.

"I said the doctor is a woman. Dr. Amy Sherwood."

The four-wheeler swerved once more, although the road was straight and clear.

AMY TURNED to Fire Chief Mitch Kannon as he stepped out of the dispatch office into the station's main area. "Change of plans, ladies."

Amy glanced at her colleague, Cheryl Tierney, a trauma nurse from Courage Bay Hospital. They had both flown in from California with their two colleagues, Nate Kellison and Dana Ivie, this morning. Chief Kannon had already sent the paramedic and EMT out on calls. The chief held out an opened bag of chocolates, but both women shook their heads. For Amy, the adrenaline had already kicked in. She hadn't been able to get down the homemade cinnamon buns the chief's daughter had brought the volunteers before the call came in about the woman in labor. Fortunately Amy's colleagues had had no problem enjoying them.

"Sheriff would like to swing by, take you, Doc, out to the high school with him."

"There's a problem?"

The chief unwrapped the candy, popped it in his mouth. He chewed slowly. "No problems yet, but like I told you, the school's been set up as an evacuation center and it's filling up fast. Although major injuries can be handled here, the sheriff would like you to have a look at the first-aid supplies and equipment at the school in case of minor emergencies. He should be here in a minute or so."

Cheryl Tierney, a trauma nurse, picked up a box of the supplies the team had brought with them from California. "I'll start setting up. It shouldn't take long."

"I can help you carry the supplies while I wait." Amy headed toward the other box.

"I'll get that." The chief set the bag of candy on the table and hoisted the other box. "One of my men is manning the radio until our dispatcher, Ruth, gets in. If the sheriff shows up, give me a shout," he told Amy.

As Cheryl and the chief headed for the far end of the firehouse, Amy opened her medical bag on one of the long tables near the kitchenette area. Although she knew everything was in order, she busied herself checking the bag's contents once more. She hated feeling useless. Some would interpret it as a fear of feeling helpless. When a ferret-faced second-year psych intern had done exactly that, she'd told him to save his analysis for rounds.

The chief came back into the station house. "Sheriff didn't show up yet?"

Amy shook her head.

"He should be right here."

Amy counted bandages by twos.

"The oddsmakers are saying Damon will turn south, come ashore down by the border. Say it'll peter out over the sea, bringing in no more than heavy rains and high winds by the time it makes landfall."

"Is that what you think, Chief?" Amy checked the tops of several saline bottles to make sure they were secure.

"That's what I pray."

She glanced up at the chief, whose blue eyes didn't miss a trick. Over six feet tall and with a width as much muscle as fat, he easily earned his title. The humbling touch of silver at his temples and the wink he now gave her told Amy he was a man who could comfort as well as command.

"I hope your prayer is answered, Chief." She turned back to her bag.

"You should sit, Doc, while you have the chance."

She hadn't come here to sit. She was used to taking care of others, not the other way around. She appreciated the chief's concern though. "Thanks, Chief, but I had my share of sitting on the flight down." She flashed him a reassuring smile and turned her attention back to her supplies for a final time. She was zipping the bag closed when she heard a new voice behind her.

"Hey, Mitch."

She stopped.

"Hey, Sheriff. How's the roads?"

"Not bad if you stay off the main routes. You ought to see the lines stretching out of the stores, though."

Amy listened to the voice. Her body was still.

"Bet by noon there's not an unbought jug of water or case of beer in the whole county," the chief said.

"Turning Point residents may be stubborn but they aren't stupid." A low chuckle came from the newcomer. Something clutched inside Amy.

She swung around, looked directly into the newcomer's eyes. A fiercer blue than the chief's, deep and dark as midnight dreams, revealing even less.

"Sheriff, this is Dr. Amy Sherwood," Mitch said. "Flew into Christi this morning with the others from Courage Bay to give us a hand. Doc, Sheriff Jesse Boone."

Amy heard the name. It repeated inside her. She felt dizzy. She forced herself to breathe, told herself it could not be. Just as swiftly she asked, *could it be?* Could this man before her be the boy she'd loved? Her mind said no. Her heart begged yes. She forbade herself to remember. She'd had fourteen years to forget.

Still, she was about to whisper, "Jess?" when the newcomer touched his hat brim and said without expression, "Ma'am." Their eyes locked. Neither one of them moved.

She didn't answer. All she could do was stare at him, her eyes ruthlessly searching. He did not turn away.

The face was not ugly, nor was it handsome. It was rugged and scarred as though once shattered and stripped and put back together. The features were slightly asymmetrical, and the skin stretched tight along the jaw, leaving no appearance of softness. Her professional eye saw that the necessary procedures had been numerous and painstaking. Her personal eye saw a strength in the jagged facial lines and the set of bones that came from the man, not modern medicine.

She saw a stranger.

"Nice to meet you, Sheriff."

She offered her hand. He didn't hesitate to take it but his touch was light. She felt the thick pad of his palm, the skin worn by hard work. She looked down at their clasped hands, felt heat flood her face. Just as if it were fourteen years ago.

"Call me Jesse, ma'am." His voice was as rough as the hand she held.

"Thank you…" She raised her eyes to the scarred face and said too softly, "Jess."

Something sparked in those blue eyes before they went flat again. His features masked, he let go of her.

"Is that your equipment?" He nodded toward the table behind her. When she nodded back, he started toward it. His gait did not reveal that his injuries had gone beyond his face, although she suspected they had. He had the admirable height of the boy she'd known, but not his bulk. Beneath his clothing, this man's body was sleek. He picked up her bag, his arms whipcord muscles and taut sinew, the fit of his uniform indicating the rest of him followed suit. A body honed to its lean limits. Whatever had been broken had been mended. Only his haunted eyes as he turned and looked at her told Amy this man had not healed.

"Anything else you need to take with you?" he asked.

She shook her head as she reached for the bag. "I can carry it."

"Not a problem, Doc." He turned to Mitch, whose own keen blue eyes had been on the couple. "Coffee, milk, sandwiches, other supplies are being brought into the high school. The traffic's heavy on the main routes, but most are heading farther inland to Laredo or the San Antonio area. But with every motel in the county full already, the high school is starting to fill up. We can accommodate a few hundred, more if necessary."

"The women's auxiliary are gathering blankets, flashlights, batteries, board games—anything that can help. As soon as they're done, they'll be over to help."

Jesse nodded. "I'll take the doctor over now."

Both men looked at Amy. She had not moved. The fire chief glanced at Jesse, but Jesse's gaze stayed on Amy.

"Ready, Doc?"

Gentleness had slipped into that last syllable. Amy doubted he intended it to be voiced. Annoyance flashed across his face, confirming her suspicion, darkening his features. She had not considered she might tumble until then. Whether the man before her was the boy she'd known fourteen years ago did not seem to matter. One soft, simple address, and her heart knew a loss she had thought long buried.

She had no choice but to move toward him. He waited until she passed him, then followed her. He reached around her to open the door and held it as she walked outside. The sun had not welcomed them when she and the rest of the Courage Bay team arrived in Turning Poont, only a heat that wrapped around, sat heavy on a body. Thickening clouds had come, and the winds were picking up.

The sheriff set her bag in the back of the Bronco, which was already stocked with a first-aid kit, flashlights, flares, blankets, jugs of water. A surge of wind came up, spun around them. They both looked to the sky as if seeking answers, saw the low, gray stillness that hovered before a hard rain. The air felt almost prickly, a smell of dust and clay in the breeze.

"We'd better go," Jesse said. The gruffness had come back into his voice as if he felt uncomfortable. His face remained impassive.

She climbed into the red-and-white vehicle with the star across the driver's door. In the cab's narrow space, she became even more aware of the man beside her, his size, his warmth, his smell like a new day. He put the vehicle into gear.

"So, how long have you been sheriff of Turning Point?"

"I was assigned three years ago to the county satellite office over at the town hall."

He answered her questions, his gaze forward. She studied his features, which were shadowed by a black Stetson.

"I thought the good guys got to wear the white hat."

He looked at her, his eyes navy-blue beneath the hat's brim. Something stirred deep inside her.

"I've met a lot of good guys. Never saw one of them with a white hat." He turned out of the firehouse parking lot, avoiding the main route in favor of a less-traveled back road.

"I once knew someone named Jesse Boone. He didn't wear a white hat either."

He glanced at her a second longer this time. She'd caught the surprise in his eyes before they went blank again. He said nothing. The firm set of his mouth caused the thin scar along his jaw to stand out in relief. The radio was tuned to the weather channel. The National Weather Service reported Damon's leading edge was two hundred miles from the coast. Seventy-five miles back it had wavered ninety degrees and started inching south. At fifty miles it had done the same. But each time it had come back to the northwest course.

"It was a long time ago I knew Jesse Boone. Fourteen years. I was a teenager. So was he."

The man's eyes stayed locked on the road, his mouth tight. He shrugged. "I suppose the name Jesse, even Boone, isn't uncommon. At least not here in Texas."

"This Jesse Boone lived in Washington for a while. I grew up there in a small town outside of Seattle. He moved there my junior year, went to my high school. He left senior year." She was silent for a moment. "I never saw him again."

Jesse couldn't look at her. She was beautiful still, with her thick brown hair and delicate build that belied a strength and determination that most people only aspired to. He'd driven to the firehouse, telling himself he could handle this. Amy would recognize the name but not the man. The plastic surgery required because of his injuries had altered his features so even he had had to look twice in the mirror for a long time. She would be in Turning Point a few days at the most until the worst of the disaster was over. Then she would return to California to her life…to her husband.

He could handle it. He'd had himself convinced. Then he'd walked into the station and looked into those eyes. Those soft turquoise eyes.

And there, less than five feet away, was the dream that had dominated his life.

The silence stretched out between them. Frustrated, Amy turned to the window, focusing on the Texas town passing by. She knew Turning Point, like all small towns, was defined by its inhabitants as much as by its warm creeks and catfish ponds—people who were born here, who grew up here, whose stubbornness and self-righteousness stemmed from a deep sense of place and community. She doubted that any of them, even if ordered, would head to higher grounds.

"Is this your first time in Texas?"

The sheriff surprised her. He did not seem one for small talk. Amy wondered if he was deliberately changing the subject. Or like her, did he need a distraction from the thoughts churning inside his head?

"Yes, it is."

"Shame it's a storm that brings you here." He did not look at her.

"Believe me, living on the California coast, we have more than our share of wild weather. A storm only a few months back had Courage Bay Hospital packed. Ever been to California?" She steered the conversation back to him.

"No, ma'am."

"Please..." She lifted her hand to touch his bare forearm. It was the first time she'd ever hesitated. "Call me Amy." She dropped her hand in her lap.

"No, I've never been to California, Amy."

It was his first lie. Jesse knew there would be many more before the disaster was over.

"Did you grow up here in Turning Point?" She continued to question him.

He kept his profile to her. His hands gripped the wheel as if he were fighting the wind. "My family has a farm here."

"Lived here your whole life?" She too could have easily been making small talk.

"I've seen some other parts of the world. Turning Point is home."

"And you've been sheriff here about three years?"

"Yes, ma'am...Amy," he corrected himself.

"Do you like the job?"

"Yes."

Amy smiled, unfazed. She was used to difficult patients. Some would even say she relished the challenge. "What do you like about it?"

He breathed in as if suppressing a sigh. "These are good people in Turning Point. I like helping them. How 'bout you? You like being a doctor?"

Counterstrike, she thought. "It's all I ever wanted to do." She'd been born with an innate need to help others, a need reinforced fourteen years ago when she'd discovered it was safer to care for others than to let someone care for you.

His gaze shifted to her. There was something undefinable in his features. "Is being a doctor everything you dreamed it would be?" he asked quietly.

It was not the usual question asked by someone she had known only five minutes. She didn't answer right away, as if considering the question for the first time herself. She was competent and not without compassion, but she was cautious with her emotions. Many of her colleagues envied her detachment, a skill necessary not only for success but for survival in the medical world. Amy feared she would never love again.

She looked at the man beside her, thought of the boy she'd loved as she studied this man who bore the same name. As if her thoughts compelled him, he looked her way. Their gazes locked.

"Lots of things don't turn out the way you expect them."

Something shifted in his eyes. The blue stone splintered. She glimpsed a longing, ageless and deep. A longing she herself had known.

Could it be?

He turned away, taking whatever she'd imagined with him. She turned back to the contours of the land, the ground hard from the August sun, the heat in the air as thick as fog.

And told herself no.

She had not acted the fool since she was eighteen. At thirty-two, she had no intention of doing so again.

JESSE HAD FEARED he could not break the gaze. He'd seen the confusion, the plea in her expression as she'd searched his face. God help him, for a second he'd prayed. *See me.*

He dragged his gaze away, saw the fresh skid marks farther up, careening from the left to the right side where the road pitched down. He slowed, saw the mid-sized car upside-down, tilted against a tree trunk. He called the accident in as he veered to the shoulder and slammed the engine into Park. Before the Bronco came to a complete stop, Jesse and Amy leapt out of the vehicle and were scrambling down the ditch's steep slope. They heard the scream as they reached the vehicle.

"Mommy!"

A blond-haired girl not more than three, strapped in a safety seat, hung upside-down in the back of the car. The vehicle must have rolled over several times. The front half of the roof was creased in, and the driver's door was crumpled. The child, seated on the opposite side, was trapped in a pocket formed between the front seat and the side of the car crushed against the tree. The child writhed against the seat constraints, terrified but appearing unharmed. An unconscious young woman was slumped half on the front seat, half on the floor, wedged in beneath the dashboard. Fluid leaking from the front of the vehicle formed a slick puddle across the ground. A thin rise of smoke snaked from the hood.

The child screamed again.

The car was a two-door. Jesse wrestled with the driver's door but the mangled metal wouldn't budge. The smoke was thickening.

He looked around. Grabbing a large rock, he slammed it against the side window until the glass shattered. "The mother is blocking the way to the girl. We'll get her out," Jesse said as he crawled through the window. "Then the child."

Smoking engine...gas leaking from the vehicle.

The child screamed again.

Amy saw several small flames shoot out from beneath the front hood as Jesse pushed his way into the car. He slipped his arm beneath the woman's arms and pulled. The woman moaned, semi-conscious, incoherent. She fought against Jesse's grasp. Suddenly an anguished cry came from her lips. Her struggling movements stopped. The woman was injured. Fortunately her twisting and writhing indicated her spine was intact.

"Don't fight me. Help me," Jesse told the woman as he pulled her from the wreckage. Small flames flared from beneath the car's hood. He felt a resistance, saw her leg was pinned beneath the dashboard. He pulled harder but he needed more leverage to free the limb. The woman's body, in response to the pain, had gone limp again. He released her and eased himself out of the car. He heard the child crying in the back.

"Her leg is pinned," he told Amy. Bracing his weight against the vehicle, he leaned as far into the car as he could and gripped the woman again under the arms. He pulled. The body resisted. He widened his stance, took a deep breath of hot air and smoke, and with an animal howl, he yanked on the woman with all his might. The body broke free. Jesse dragged the woman until he could take her into his arms and carry her several yards away. As he laid her on the hard ground, he saw her leg was twisted at an odd angle, the bone popped out of the flesh.

"Amy," he yelled. He turned back to the car and saw Amy crawl into it.

The child screamed for its mother as Amy approached her. "It's all right. Everything's going to be fine." Amy continued the reassurances even though the child could not hear her, knowing they were as much for her as the girl. Behind her, she heard Jesse ordering her out of there, swearing as she ignored him. She could hear the flames licking beneath the hood. She pushed herself up. Pain shot up her thigh as her knee pressed into something sharp. She pushed herself into the narrow opening in the back, twisting her body to shield the child. She unclasped the safety belt, the child kicking against the restraints and Amy. She pulled the girl toward her, clasping her against her chest as she slid out of the tight space. The inside of the car was radiating heat. Strange popping noises came from beneath the hood. She twisted, pressing the splinter of glass deeper into her knee. She passed the child to Jesse. He hugged the child to his chest and held her with one arm. His other arm reached for Amy.

"Take my hand."

"Go," she screamed.

He reached in, gripped her arm and yanked her toward him. Her foot had slipped and was caught between the console and the passenger seat. She heard a loud *whoosh.* Flames leaped from the engine skyward, receded.

"Go," she screamed.

Jesse turned away. Someone else must have arrived at the scene, because when he turned back, the child was gone from his arms. "I'm not leaving you." Both his hands reached in, grabbed her upper arms. The heat was like a living thing now. Amy felt her head going light. Fresh flames surged, higher, closer. Jesse crawled into the car, the sweat streaking his face.

"Get out!" she screamed.

He moved toward her, his hands reaching until they slid around her. She heard him expel a breath, then inhale sharply as he jerked her toward him. Her body lurched forward an inch, then resisted. He twisted her torso toward him and yanked again. She gasped for oxygen, black spots dancing in front of her eyes. She blinked, struggling against the blackness. Jesse's face came into focus. His hat was gone, she realized. She would buy him a new one. A white one.

Then the world exploded.

CHAPTER TWO

SHE LANDED on top of Jesse, their bodies hitting the earth with a thud, a scream dying on her lips. He wrapped his arms around her, holding her tight against his chest. For several moments, they did not move, but lay there like two lovers. Amy lifted her head, looked down at the man beneath her. The tip of her tongue moistened her dry lips. The muscles in the man's throat rippled as he swallowed. Men's terse voices sounded at the edges of her consciousness. They were not alone.

"Thank you," she whispered. *Whoever you are,* she thought. She rolled off him and sat up, dusting herself off. Trickles of blood from the cut on her knee had already dried on her leg.

Jesse sat up beside her, looked at her leg with concern. "You cut yourself." His hand curved around her calf as he leaned over to inspect the injury.

"Just a small cut." Her voice trembled at his touch. He raised his gaze to her and their eyes met. She swallowed.

"You two all right?"

Jesse drew back from Amy. Mitch Kannon looked down at them. Firemen had extinguished the flames of the burning car before the wind spread the fire. Their hoses, fed by the pumper truck and fat with pressure, were still aimed at the car, giving it a final wash.

Jesse looked up at the chief. "I could use a beer."

He stood, reached for Amy and pulled her up beside him. "I'm fine, Chief," she assured Mitch.

"She cut her knee," Jesse pointed out.

"Nothing tweezers, a little disinfectant and a Band-Aid won't take care of," Amy insisted. "In fact, I'm going to get my bag now and do exactly that."

She walked over and picked up her medical kit, but instead of treating herself, continued to the young mother flat on a stretcher as emergency workers stabilized her leg.

"She's a spitfire, that one," Mitch noted, casting a sidelong glance at Jesse.

She always was, Jesse thought. "The mother say anything about how they landed upside-down in a ditch?"

"The child was drinking from her sippy cup—"

"Her what?"

"Sippy cup. One of those small plastic cups with a cover and spout so kids don't spill their juice. You know?"

Jesse looked blankly at the fire chief.

"That's right," Mitch said. "You don't have kids. Well, when you do, you'll bless the person who invented the sippy cup. Anyhow, the kid dropped hers, and the mother, fearing it was still full and was leaking all over the floor, reached into the back but couldn't find it. She swears she turned her head for just a second to see if she could see where it rolled. When she turned back, she was heading to the other side of the road. Panicking, she twisted the wheel too hard, losing control of the car as it hit the shoulder."

Jesse expelled a breath. "Thank God no one was killed."

"Someone could have been."

Jesse caught Mitch's glance.

"I don't know if jumping into a burning car like that is the most heroic or the most moronic thing I've ever seen two people do," the chief said.

"We got them out." Jesse watched Amy as she squatted beside the child, who was lying on a stretcher next to her mom. She'd unclipped the stuffed frog on her stethoscope and slipped it on her finger. She moved it slowly across the child's line of vision, testing the girl's responses. She smiled when done. The stuffed frog did a jig atop Amy's finger before it grazed the child's cheek in a pretend kiss. The girl broke into a smile, the anxiety erased from her young features.

Pride surged through Jesse. He'd always known Amy would be a great doctor. She'd been brilliant as well as beautiful. He, on the other hand, had been nothing but brawn and brash, born with a natural athletic ability that he'd known was his only ticket to a college education. Until the accident…

He looked at Amy and her patient. He did not regret the decision he'd made fourteen years ago. Nor the one he had made minutes ago.

"In the future—" Mitch's voice cut into his thoughts. "Try to stay out of burning cars about to blow. The world doesn't have enough good men. Or women," he added. "We can't afford to lose two more."

Jesse half smiled as he watched Amy. "I can't promise you anything. Especially with that one. She puts her mind to something, best you just get out of her way."

"Sounds like you know her pretty well."

His eyes met the chief's. "Just an observation."

The chief smiled. "Same here."

Mitch headed toward his men. Jesse walked over to Amy and her patient. "Hey, Sunshine." He squatted at eye-level with the child. "Not only are you the most beautiful little one I've ever seen, I believe you're the bravest."

The child smiled shyly, averting her gaze.

"Your mommy and you are going to be just fine." He glanced at Amy for confirmation. She nodded.

The rescue workers came over to the child. "She'll ride with her mother?" Jesse asked. The men nodded.

"These nice men are going to give you and your mommy a ride in a big shiny car, Sunshine. Do you like ice cream?"

The child nodded.

"Chocolate?"

The girl shook her head. "B'nilla," she said.

Jesse's smile widened. "Well, these two men are going to make sure you get all the *b'nilla* ice cream you can handle. Deal?" He offered his hand.

Her eyes round and solemn, the girl put her small hand into Jesse's and nodded.

"Ice cream!" The stuffed frog, his voice supplied sotto voce by Amy, nuzzled the girl's cheek once more. "I love ice cream. Can I come, too? Huh, can I?" The frog danced atop Amy's finger.

Smiling, the girl nodded. Amy unclipped the stuffed animal and attached it to the girl's T-shirt. "Freddy, you're so lucky to have a friend as pretty and brave as Caroline. She'll take good care of you." Amy leaned in, pecked the stuffed animal, then the girl, on the cheek. The girl smiled. Amy and Jesse waved as the rescue workers carried the child away.

Amy nodded.

"How you doing?" Jesse asked.

She gave him a sidelong glance. "I could use a beer."

For the first time, Jesse Boone smiled at her.

"How 'bout a Band-Aid?" he said, glancing at her knee. "And a cup of coffee?"

"IN ADDITION to powerful winds, Hurricane Damon is expected to spin off destructive tornadoes, drench the region with up to ten inches of rainfall and hit the coast with a storm surge that could measure ten to fifteen feet." The veteran forecaster on the diner's television screen leaned toward the camera. "Evacuation and preparation times are diminishing."

Amy and Jesse walked toward the counter at the far end of the diner, but neither sat on the cracked leatherette stools. A few customers were seated in the booths that lined the wall, but most of the patrons sat at the counter, backs hunched, elbows propped. Several glanced away from the television screen to give Jesse a nod hello. Their gazes flickered questioningly at Amy before the weather report consumed their attention again.

"Interstates are closed to all shorebound traffic.

While coastal residents are making their way inland to evacuation shelters inside schools, churches and courthouses—" the screen flashed an aerial view of traffic snaking its way up the highway "—inland residents are stocking up on water, batteries, candles, matches, nonperishables and kerosene." The screen filled with equally long lines at checkout aisles.

Jesse raised a halting hand to the waitress as she set thick white cups before Amy and him. "Make it to go, darlin'."

Ignoring the sheriff, the waitress poured from the pot she wielded with the expertise of a professional gun slinger. "Can't live on caffeine in a cardboard cup, Sheriff. That storm isn't going to do much in the time it takes to fill your stomach.

Jesse looked at Amy.

"The chief's daughter brought us home-made cinnamon rolls when we got to the station."

Jesse smiled. "I thought I smelled them. Figured it was just wishful thinking."

"I only had coffee, though. I have a hard time choking anything else down before noon."

"That settles it, Sheriff." The waitress slapped menus on the counter.

"You are right, darlin'. As always."

The waitress smiled. "You learned a long time ago not to argue with me, didn't you, Sheriff?"

"Or any woman, for that matter," Jesse said as he slid on the stool and raised the steaming cup to his lips.

One of the men seated at the counter, watching the television screen with a satellite picture of the gulf, an angry-looking orange-red mass in the middle, turned to them. "I say it slows, veers south, burning itself down to rain and wind by the time it hits the coast. What do you think, Sheriff?"

Jesse watched the screen. "Never been a gambling man, Gunther."

He regretted the words as soon as they left his mouth. A simple off-the-cuff remark. Unless, of course, your father had been Jesse Boone, Senior, a man who, once the sun rose in the morning, would have taken odds on whether it'd set that night. Jesse sipped the steaming black brew and was not disappointed by the bitterness that bit the back of his throat. Amy's gaze turned his way and again he cursed his own stupidity. Behind those gorgeous green eyes, he feared the wheels were turning.

He'd arrived in Amy's town a bad boy, "troubled teen," the child welfare worker would term it, but unlike his father, he'd always stopped short of breaking any "official" laws. Still, he'd grown up with the guilt of the wrongs his father had done. His career choice was obviously one way to atone for his father's sins. He didn't need a hundred-fifty-dollar-an-hour shrink to figure that one out.

And Amy, her eyes still on him, sure as hell didn't either.

"Darlin'?"

Amy looked blankly at the waitress. Her thoughts were a lifetime away on the teenager who'd rolled into a small Washington town with his father and no mention of other family or roots. Suspicion from the townspeople at the sheer fact that he was a stranger was a given, and the boy had done little to calm their fears. On the contrary, with his wild ways and sexy looks, Jesse Boone had seemed determined to prove the townspeople right. But Amy had believed in him, even after people cursed his father for moving on with their deposits for contracted repairs never begun. Jesse wasn't his father, Amy had told herself. He didn't break promises. No one could convince her otherwise. Until one night, dressed in her senior prom gown, which had cost her mother far too much, she'd waited until dawn for a boy who never came.

"Coffee, right, Doc?" the sheriff asked her, bringing her back to the present.

The waitress waited patiently. A name plate pinned above a well-supported bosom read Lurie.

"I'm sorry," Amy said.

"No problem, honey." The waitress hoisted the pot from hip level, angled it toward Amy. "Coffee?"

Amy looked at the inky black liquid and shook her head. "Just herbal tea, please. And honey if you have a jar in the back."

"Uh-oh," Jesse muttered into his cup as the waitress rocked back on her heels and gave Amy a good once-over. "There goes your cover."

"You're from the California crew that came in from Christi this morning, aren't you, darlin'?"

"Lurie, this is Dr. Amy Sherwood," Jesse introduced.

The waitress shifted the coffeepot to her other hand and extended the free one. "Welcome to Turning Point, Doc."

Amy took the hand with its inch-long fingernails decorated with silver crescent moons. "Thank you. I'm glad I could come in to lend a hand."

"Not as happy as we are. Now, let me get your tea, but between me and you, darlin'—" the waitress leaned in "—I'd get the caffeine in my system while I can."

The waitress moved on down the counter without waiting for a reply, refilling mugs before she set the coffeepot back on the burner plate.

"There was Bret in '99, but that was mainly wind and rain by the time it came in to Christi," a man several stools away was saying.

But Amy's thoughts went much farther back. Fourteen years back to when Coach Lasher had called her into the athletic office and asked her to tutor one of the football players. It was Coach Lasher who'd clocked Jesse in phys ed at a six-minute mile and saw a natural quarterback in the boy's speed and grace. Coach Lasher also knew the exercise would help to channel the boy's restless energy, relieve an inner anger that seemed to burn through him; the practices and structure of the sport would help to teach the boy discipline. But as well as the boy did in athletics, he did poorly in school work. School policy stated no athlete failing a subject could compete in sports. Jesse was failing three. Amy, president of the National Honor Society, tutored classmates during study hall. She hadn't known the term *dyslexia* then. All she knew was that Jesse had a hard time reading, studying gave him tremendous headaches, and many times he wrote his letters backwards. He'd been called lazy and stupid for so long, he'd believed it was the truth. Amy showed him otherwise. For the first time, he'd wanted something so badly he'd put in the hours of frustration and work. Amy thought it was football he wanted. Later she learned it was her. They were together one year, and she'd loved him so deeply, the memory of it slammed her heart against her chest.

Lurie brought her tea but Amy kept her gaze on the man beside her. She looked at him so hard the waitress copied her pose. He turned away from the weather coverage and faced her, allowing her to study him openly. If it was the Jesse Boone she'd loved all those years ago, they both knew he owed her that much.

Was it him? Amy asked herself for what must be the hundredth time that day. Was it the man to whom she'd once freely given her heart, too young to know any better, too blinded by love to heed her mother's warnings? She looked for an answer. Was it him?

And what if it was? What then?

Lurie pulled a jar of honey out of a deep apron pocket and set it down on the counter with a slight bang. Amy started.

"There's your honey, honey." Lurie flashed a smile. "The usual, Sheriff?" Her smile widened. Her turquoise eye shadow had settled into the creases of her eyelids but the candy-apple red on her lips had a fresh sheen.

Jesse nodded. Lurie scribbled something on a small green pad, glanced at Amy, her pencil poised above the pad.

"Doc?"

Amy looked at the plastic coated menu. "I'll have a grilled cheese sandwich, please. Could you put a slice of tomato on it?"

Lurie nodded, noting it on her pad.

"On whole wheat if you have it."

Lurie nodded again.

"And I'd prefer Swiss cheese instead of American."

Lurie looked up at her.

"If you have it."

"We have it."

"And instead of fries, could I have extra coleslaw on the side? In a separate dish so the dressing doesn't spread to the sandwich and make it soggy?"

"Not a problem. Anything else?" Lurie's pencil tapped the pad.

"An extra pickle?"

Lurie was shaking her head as she took their orders into the kitchen.

"I can't help it," Amy said as she swiveled toward Jesse. "I love dill pickles."

Jesse's head tipped to the side as he looked at her, an amused smile on his face.

Amy sighed. "I know. High-maintenance."

"Seems like a control issue to me." Jesse sipped his coffee, amusement still lighting the usual dark cast of his eyes.

"Really?" Amy smiled. She picked up her own cup of tea. "Of course, you're right."

"Of course I am." He teased her easily.

"A symptom of that whole physician-as-god complex."

"Exactly what I was thinking." He was so handsome when he smiled. His eyes softened. His mouth curved, became accessible.

Amy looked away. "That's what brings ninety percent of us to medical school in the first place. Joke's on us when we learn that nine times out of ten, things are out of our control."

"That's not just in the medical field, Doc. That's life in general."

Amy stirred her tea, smiled. "Still, it doesn't seem to stop us from trying like hell."

He surprised her by clinking his cup against hers.

"I upset Lurie, didn't I?" Her smile faded.

"I think it was the extra pickle that broke her."

She laughed softly, finding it easy to laugh with him. "She has a crush on you."

"You trying to make me blush, Doc?"

"Is that possible?"

"We big, burly protectors of society have our sensitive sides."

She liked seeing him smile. Not a polite smile, but one that relieved the flatness of his eyes and revealed warmth underneath.

"So…?" She angled a questioning gaze at him.

"So…what?"

Amy cocked her head toward Lurie at the far end of the counter. "So…" She aimed a pointed look at his hands, bare of rings. "I'm assuming you're single if you're going to flirt with pretty waitresses. If not, my illusion of a real-life Texas sheriff is going to be forever crushed."

"Some might say my marital status is not exactly a pertinent issue here."

"Is that a polite way of saying it's none of my damn business?"

"In true Texas-sheriff fashion."

She laughed, and he joined her. The scars stretched and faded. The pain that held his features tight eased. His laughter was like that of the boy she'd known, but then she'd heard a thousand similar laughs over the last fourteen years—across a room, on the street, in her dreams. For a moment, she was eighteen again and still believed all her desires would come true.

They were still laughing as Lurie arrived with their food. Amy saw the looks pass beneath the billed baseball caps of the men seated nearby, but she didn't care. Right now, cows were lying flat in the fields and the rodents had burrowed for cover. Plywood strips were being fastened across windows and doors with three-inch nails. Generators were being checked, rugs rolled and pressed tight to doorjambs. Yet no one could ever be ready for what was to come. So for a few minutes at this counter, she would laugh with a man who bore the same name as a boy she had loved.

"Here you go." Lurie set plates before them. Jesse's "usual" was a king-size cheeseburger, a side of onion rings and a double chocolate shake. Lurie slipped a bottle of Tabasco sauce out of her apron pocket, put it beside his plate. Amy stopped smiling. She'd known only one other person in her lifetime who put hot sauce on his hamburger. She watched him unscrew the top, lift up the bun and splash the sauce on his burger. He replaced the bun, brought the burger to his mouth and took a big bite. He glanced at her untouched plate. “Something wrong?” he asked, chewing.

“The hot sauce on your hamburger…” She didn’t know what she was trying to say.

“Heavenly.” He took another big bite. “Obviously one of those true Texan habits that hasn’t hit the West Coast yet.” He tipped his head. Amy looked around. At every station, a similar bottle of hot sauce stood beside the catsup bottle. “Of course, when it does, you Californians will claim you all started the trend and take the credit.”

Amy smiled wanly, feeling foolish. She looked down at her food, but her appetite was gone.

“So, you’re married?” she asked bluntly.

He seemed to have trouble swallowing. “No, I’m not. Your image of a true Texas sheriff may remain intact.” He picked up an onion ring. “And I, darlin’, am free to flirt with whomever I want.”

Jesse didn’t ask if she were married. He didn’t have to. Still, sitting beside her, he wondered if she’d ever dreamed the things he had in the years they’d been apart. Had she dreamed of them holding each other, kissing in the soft moonlight? Dreamed of their naked bodies…?

He leaned back, wiped his mouth and dropped the napkin onto his empty plate. “Excuse me.” He rose from the counter and headed to the rest room.

Amy watched him, too many questions still forming in her mind. Lurie came over and picked up Jesse’s plate. Amy turned to her, pushed her own plate toward the edge of the counter. Lurie looked at the half-eaten sandwich as she stacked the plate atop the other. "Was everything okay?"

"Oh, yes, fine," Amy assured her. "I'm just not terribly hungry."

Lurie cocked a hip, balancing both plates in one hand as she gathered used napkins and Amy's empty glass in the other. "I've been trying to get the sheriff to smile like that for two years."

Amy looked at her, interested.

"Hell's bells, half the single women in the county have been trying to get their claws into the good sheriff."

"He doesn't date?"

"Oh, he dates all right. Probably been through most of the single women in a twenty-mile radius and then some."

"He's charming…" Amy noted.

Lurie crossed her arms across her arresting bosom and gave a slow nod of agreement.

"But he doesn't strike me as the playboy type," Amy concluded.

Lurie leaned on the counter, settling in. "That's exactly the problem, Doc. He's a real gentleman and a wonderful date, but if things start heating up, getting too serious, he slows it down or calls it quits altogether. He refuses to go to the next level."

"You and he…?"

Lurie nodded. "We dated. And he was upfront about what to expect from the first. He didn't lead me on. He'll let you know he enjoys your company and treats you right, but if a woman is looking for the cozy cottage and the rest of the enchilada, she's got the wrong man. Of course, like most woman, I thought I could change him." She paused, studied her fingertips with their crescent moons. "I didn't." She met Amy's gaze.

"A lot of men are afraid of commitment, settling down, Lurie."

Lurie shook her head. "It's different with Jesse. I can't explain. It's like he lives with a ghost. When we were dating, he'd look at me, but I sensed he was looking at someone else. Or for someone else. And no matter how hard he looked, he couldn't find her."

The waitress straightened. "At least, not yet." She gave Amy a wink, swiveled and sauntered into the kitchen, her hips swaying beneath her tight black skirt.

Jesse returned. He stood beside her stool. "Lurie giving you some good gossip?" He threw several bills down on the counter.

"Just girl talk," Amy answered as she slid off the stool.

"She's a good gal," Jesse said as they moved toward the door. He nodded good-bye to the other customers. "But believe about fifty percent of what she says."

"How do you know she didn't say the same about you?"

"She probably said believe only ten percent of what I say."

"Actually, she said you were a straight shooter. She's a big fan. Like most of the single women in the county."

Their eyes met. "Is that what she said?"

"That and some."

He slowly shook his head, laughing under his breath.

"You don't agree?"

He reached across her to the door, so close she could feel his warmth, sense his strength.

"You'll have me blushing yet, darlin'," he said in a low voice that made Amy hold her breath. She stepped away, through the door, and exhaled.

The clouds were denser and darker. The winds that had come were rougher, quicker, their hard edges hitting a person dead on. Rain broke through the sky with a furor that laid the field grass flat.

"Wait here," Jesse told Amy beneath the shelter of the diner's metal awning. "I'll get the Bronco and pick you up."

He was gone before Amy could protest. She watched him weave his way among the other vehicles in the parking lot. The drop in barometric pressure could cause joints to swell, deepen aches from past injuries. If that was the case, there was no indication in Jesse's movements.

When the Bronco pulled up in front of the diner, Amy hurried to meet it even as Jesse jumped out the driver's side and was rounding the vehicle to open the door for her.

True Texas-sheriff fashion, she thought as he swung open the door. She turned to thank him and found him close. She pushed back the hair the wind whipped across her face and gathered it in one hand. Her other hand clung to the side of the vehicle, steadying her while the wind and the rain and something equally elemental and powerful seemed to push her toward this man.

Jesse stepped back. He shut the door on her as she climbed inside. Her face turned to his, its questioning stare now blurred by the rivulets of rain across the window. The breath he released was a long shudder as he rounded to the driver's door.

Inside the vehicle, the dark sky and rain pounding hard on the roof created an intimacy, closing them off from the outside world.

"Jesse?"

He felt her hand on his forearm, a thousand longings in the feel of her fingertips alone. She'd said his name too softly and with too much question. He feared to turn and look into those blue-green eyes that he had dreamt about for fourteen years, afraid that if she asked, he would not lie. He would tell her the truth and damn the consequences.

He looked down at her small hand on his arm. The ripple of a scar on his own flesh returned him to his senses. If she asked, he could say he was not the Jesse Boone she had known fourteen years ago. Nor was she the young girl he'd taken in his arms and loved with every ounce of his soul. Too many years had passed, too much time and too many changes had come between them, conspired to keep them apart.

He raised his gaze to her. She searched his face.

A dispatcher's voice over the radio interrupted.

"Fire reported in the old fertilizer warehouse over by the railroad station. Pickup truck traveling at high speed skidded off the highway. The truck was carrying kerosene and exploded on impact. County emergency vehicles en route."

Jesse switched on the lights, the siren and punched the gas pedal.

Disaster had begun.

CHAPTER THREE

THEY SMELLED the smoke before they saw it. One pumper truck was already on the scene. Another arrived. Six men jumped out and started unwinding the hose. The building, a two-story barn built before the newer fabricated steel structures came into favor, had been abandoned three years ago when the business closed down. Flames, fueled by the kerosene and the warehouse's debris, raged through the lower floor.

Amy pulled out a vinyl poncho from the back of the van, grabbed her bag and moved through the rain toward the scene. Any advantage provided by the rain was cancelled out by the wind feeding the flames. Deep, terse voices sliced the air. A man in a heavy slick coat, boots and helmet took the first folds of the hose; others followed. The white snaking hose grew fat with pressure. Water streamed from the nozzle into the building, the crackling of the fire now joined by the steaming and hissing of wet wood falling.

"Give me some more line," a man yelled. Amy saw Jesse grab gear off the hook-and-ladder, pulling boots to thighs, clipping coatrings closed as he cornered the truck. Then he disappeared among the others, identical in their protective uniforms. The fire surged in its fight.

"I'm Dr. Amy Sherwood with the Courage Bay emergency team that came in this morning," she shouted above the wind and rain to a squad member. "Where's the driver?" She indicated the blackened pickup.

"Ambulance already took him to County," the man shouted back.

"Any other passengers?"

"No, just the driver."

A series of explosions inside the warehouse blew out windows. The hoses blasted the building full force.

Amy looked at the fireman. "Nitrate," he explained. "It's used in fertilizer. Must be some old bags still stored in there."

She turned to where the men leaned into the hose to relieve the pressure straining their arms. A fireman, head bowed against the falling, flaming chunks of the warehouse, ran from the back of the building with a body in his arms. The body was long, a man easily six foot but lean, and the firefighter had the width of a powerful man.

Amy rushed over, recognizing Chief Kannon as he threw off his helmet and mask. Mitch laid the man down on a portable stretcher in the back of an SUV, out of the rain. The man was unconscious, late fifties, unshaven, malnourished. His skin, like well-worn leather, had a blue-gray ashy cast.

"Bring the resuscitator," Mitch yelled.

Amy bent over the man, tilted back his head, and

breathed into his mouth, checking for chest rise. Nothing. She placed one hand over the other on the chest and pumped lightly like a heart. Sixty beats per minute.

"Don't recognize him," Mitch said. "He might have come in on the trains, holed up in the building. I found him not far from the back door. He must have been trying to get out when the smoke overcame him."

Amy leaned in to the man's tilted head, breathed. Nothing. "The airway passages are too swollen. No oxygen is getting through."

A firefighter ran over with the mechanical resuscitator. The chief began fitting the facepiece connection into the regulator.

"We've got to open the airways first." Amy reached into her bag for an emergency trach kit. With swift, precise movements, she sliced into the windpipe at the base of the throat, being careful not to touch muscle or vein. She inserted a thin tube, leaned down, breathed, watched the chest inflate.

"Give him oxygen," she told the chief. She looked up, saw a firefighter nearby whip off his helmet, and vomit on his boots.

The mechanical resuscitator forced pure oxygen into the man's lungs until they expanded and built up enough pressure to push the air out. The machine breathed for the man. His color stayed gray. She looked up and saw Jesse unstrap his helmet, his face colored with the heat of the fire, streaked with soot and his own sweat. He breathed deeply, taking in fresh air. Behind him, she saw the worst of the fire had been contained. Only one line was needed now to give the building a last bath to make sure no embers waited for the wind. The warehouse stood, hollowed and charred. The blackened truck wasn't far off, as if part of a matching set.

The resuscitator breathed. A quick, clicking sound of air in, out, in, out. "He's still not breathing on his own," Amy told Jesse and the chief. "He needs to get to a hospital."

"The rescue squad is on its way to Beeville with the burn victim—the truck driver. He belongs in Houston, but the storm has grounded the Flight for Life. We could call County."

Amy shook her head. "There's no time."

"Put him in the Bronco," Jesse said. "We'll take him to Beeville."

He and Mitch lifted the blanketed body and carried it to the sheriff's vehicle, Amy moving in unison, linked by the machine. All the while, the wind and rain tried to thwart them. Once Jesse flattened the back seat, they eased the man onto it. Amy propped herself by his side, and Mitch headed back to his crew. Jesse stripped off his gear, the rain washing him down.

"How far is the hospital?" Amy asked.

"About thirty-five miles north." Jesse climbed behind the wheel and turned on the lights and siren, heading toward the interstate.

The winds had gotten stronger. Amy could feel them playing with the van, pushing against the sides while the rain battered the roof. Her patient's pulse was weakening. "Come on, come on," she urged in the rhythm of the breathing apparatus.

"Move." Jesse's order was directed at the heavy traffic slowing their progress. He took to the shoulder where necessary. After about ten miles, the lanes began to clear. The vehicle gained speed.

Jesse radioed ahead to the hospital, and emergency personnel were waiting for them with a stretcher. Amy walked beside the stretcher, reporting on the man's condition.

"Thanks, Doc," an intern told her.

Amy nodded, then stepped away as the patient was wheeled through the hospital's double doors. She turned and found Jesse waiting for her. Their eyes met, and Amy knew the grimness in his gaze was mirrored in her own.

"C'mon," he said, the strength in his low voice calling her. "I'll buy you an herbal tea."

She shook her head and smiled wanly. "Coffee."

They opted for a convenience store over the hospital cafeteria. Both filled tall cardboard cups with black, steaming liquid, Amy adding cream and sugar. Jesse drank his black, she mentally noted. The Jesse Boone she'd known hadn't drunk coffee at all, but then again, neither had she fourteen years ago.

They moved to the cashier, their gazes drawn to the portable television behind the counter, its screen filled with mesmerizing concentric circles of blue, red, yellow. The image changed to an aerial view of traffic heading in from the coast area, then to empty store shelves.

Jesse glanced at Amy, her gaze intent on the television report. Years ago, he had resigned himself to the fact that he'd lost her forever. Now she stood beside him. He looked at the fury filling the screen. The gods were having a field day today.

> Tropical-storm-force winds extending more than 100 miles out from the hurricane's eye could cause torrential rainstorms and inland flooding as deadly and disastrous as storm-surge flooding. Tornadoes possible along the northern side of the hurricane's spiral.

"They upgraded it to a Category Four," the cashier told them as he handed them their change. The severity of hurricanes was measured on a scientific scale. Only a Category Five was worse.

A shot of the coast filled the screen. The waves rose like twenty-foot walls, rolled onto themselves, breaking into sheets of blowing white spray. Others even larger and more powerful followed. The camera panned to a plywood sheet protecting the windows of a beach shop. A black bull's-eye had been spray painted in the center, the message Hit me with your best shot, Damon…Fire away painted beside it. Neither Amy nor Jesse smiled.

They ran to the SUV, heads bowed against the force of the rain, hands curved protectively over the tops of their coffee cups. Inside the vehicle's cab, they hauled off their raincoats, spraying the interior and themselves with fat drops of water. Outside, the winds caught the rain, sweeping it hard horizontally so that the water seemed to be running up the windows instead of down.

Latest predictions were the storm would hit around midnight. It was now 4:00 p.m.

They drove in silence, sipping their coffee. Lightning flashed bright as day, slicing through the rain's curtain. The vehicle trembled with the weight of the storm. Jesse set his coffee container in the console's cup holder and held the steering wheel steady with two hands.

"Traffic heading north seems lighter," Amy noted.

"Most who evacuated have got to where they were going and settled in," Jesse said.

"The storm could still bend or even weaken before it comes ashore."

He nodded, but the way the scar stretched thin along his jaw showed anything but optimism.

"You think it'll be as bad as they say?" Amy asked.

"Hard to predict with a storm this size. It's already shifted twice. Like you said, it could shift again, veer south. A change in air patterns over the next few hours, and Damon could end up being no more than a tropical storm with heavy winds and rain."

His eyes on the road, Jesse overreached for his coffee cup and mistakenly brushed Amy's arm. Frowning, he glanced across at her. "Sorry." He wrapped his hand around the coffee cup and raised it to his lips, his gaze returning to the road. His other hand clenched the steering wheel, the emotions rising inside him as strong as the storm outside the windows. Her flesh had been soft, warm despite the lingering dampness. He set his coffee back down and took the steering wheel with both hands, struggling for control. Fourteen years later, and she could still take him with one touch.

They had left the interstate and were on a county route close to Turning Point when they saw a garbage can in the middle of the other lane. Trash bags were strewn around it, and its lid lay several feet away. Jesse pulled over to the shoulder. "I'll be right back," he said, reaching for his raincoat in the back. Amy started to do the same.

"Where you going?" he asked her.

"I'll get the lid. You get the can." She pulled on the vinyl poncho. "We can both get the garbage."

"I can handle it, thanks. You stay here." He looked up and down the road, waited for two cars to pass, then jumped out of the Bronco. He paused as a truck came too fast around the corner, steered around the trash. He was about to start across when he heard a car door slam closed. "Damn stubborn woman," he muttered, his heart growing warm. He erased his small smile before she reached his side, replacing it with a stern gaze as she fell into step beside him.

"I came here to help, Sheriff."

"You'll have plenty of opportunities for that, Doc. But if you enjoy standing out in the pouring rain, don't let me stop you."

He crossed toward the garbage can, now spinning in the wind. Amy ran to grab the lid.

"I don't enjoy standing out in the pouring rain, Sheriff," she shouted. "But I'd enjoy even less having to patch up your sorry butt if a car came around that corner too fast and struck you down."

He bent to pick up the remaining bag of garbage and hide the grin he let himself enjoy. He straightened, his features mirroring his posture until he saw her standing, arm outstretched, palm out, signaling any oncoming cars to stop. Only there weren't any cars in sight.

"What corner would that be, Doc? That treacherous one there?" He indicated a slight bend in the road that offered no possibility of obstructed view as he took the lid from her and locked it onto the trash can.

"Exactly." She stood straight, arms still outstretched to halt any cars should they come. "Not to mention impaired visibility from the rain," she yelled after him as he carried the can to a house at the side of the road. Finding the garage open, Jesse secured the garbage pail inside. "Put the two together and there's a high possibility you could be roadkill in a matter of seconds."

He headed back to her.

"Then I'd have a hell of a time explaining to the whole town what happened to their beloved local law enforcement officer," Amy shouted, "and would go down in the annals of Turning Point history as Dr. Amy Sherwood, sheriff-killer."

"Doc?"

"What?" she snapped, having worked herself up into a righteous, rain-soaked bundle of indignation unhappy about being interrupted.

"There's a car passing the one coming up in the lane behind you, so I suggest you move your butt."

Amy glanced over her shoulder, said a word she rarely used and marched back to the sheriff's vehicle.

Inside the cab, she whipped her poncho off. She unfastened her hair and wrung the wetness out of it before she twisted it up again.

Jesse slipped his own rain gear off and brushed his fingers through his wet hair. "That's okay. You don't have to thank me for saving your life. All in a day's work, ma'am."

She swung her head toward him with a restrained precision that he knew cost her. A murderous look deepened her turquoise eyes to navy. "What I'll thank you for is to leave my butt—" her teeth snapped together on the word "—out of this."

The urge to kiss those firm, full lips came so swift, so strong. He leaned toward her. Her dark eyes clouded, searched his face, looking for a man who no longer existed. He forced himself upright and put the vehicle into gear. Steering onto the road, he ignored the desire that would not go away. "It wasn't exactly a politically correct comment, was it, Doc?"

Amy sank back into the seat as if the round were over. "I started it, Sheriff."

"What would be the politically correct term for 'sorry butt?'" he teased. "Please move your genetically-uninspired gluts? They say that in California?"

He watched her face light up as she smiled. The urge to take her in his arms, press his mouth to hers spiked. His gut twisted.

"Why are we talking about butts?" she asked him.

"You're talking about butts. I'm talking about genetically—"

"Sheriff Boone," a voice interrupted over the radio. Amy stopped smiling. They both leaned forward.

"Sheriff Boone, over." Jesse replied.

"Your cousin Clare's youngest has been calling the

station, asking to speak to you. He sounds upset but he refuses to talk to anyone but you. I told him I'd get the message to you, have you contact him. You can reach him at home."

"Thanks," Jesse said to his dispatcher. "I'll give him a call."

"Better do it fast. Storm's even interfering with mobile reception."

After he signed off, Jesse pulled out his cellular phone.

"Worth a try," he told Amy.

"Would you like me to dial for you?"

"I got it. Thanks though." He punched the numbers. "Shane? Shane?" he repeated, louder. "This is your Uncle Jesse. What's wrong, kiddo?"

Amy heard the tenderness come into Jesse's voice.

"Shane? Shane?" Jesse tried twice more, then snapped off the phone and dropped it into the console, about to mutter a phrase he never used in mixed company when he stopped himself. "I lost the connection."

Amy released an expletive equal to the one he'd suppressed. "Here." She twisted over the seat into the back, and rummaged in her bag. "Use mine."

Jesse shook his head. "The winds are too strong. I'm almost to Granger's garage. I'll go in and try the phone there." He pressed on the accelerator.

He left the van running as he sprinted into the gas station. A few minutes later, he came out, the customary grimness on his face covering concern.

"What's wrong?" Amy asked as he opened the door.

"Michael, my cousin Clare's oldest boy, skipped

football practice and went down to the seashore with some other boys to take advantage of the high waves coming in from the storm. He told Shane he'd beat the tar out of him if he said anything, but it's been a few hours. It's getting late and Michael should have been back by now. Shane's been watching the weather reports and is scared big-time."

"Where's your cousin?" Amy asked.

"Clare's at work. She's a cashier at the Smart-Mart over in Driscoll. Her shift ends at five, but she just called home to say she'd be a little late. Everyone's scrambling to stock up and the lines were stretching out the door. Shane didn't want to worry her about Michael, but with the rain and the wind and the reports on the TV, he's getting nervous."

"Where's the boys' father?"

Jesse dragged a hand across his face, rubbed his forehead. "Clare's husband left her about a year ago for a younger blonde and moved to California. It's been tough on the boys, but Michael especially has been giving her a hard time. Their father had both boys out for about a month this summer, bought them surfboards. Ever since Michael's come back, he eats, sleeps and dreams surfing. Damn kids."

Amy heard his worry. She thought of her own son, home in California, safe with Aunt Betts. Still, a mother never stopped worrying.

"I'll drop you off at the high school." He switched on the turn signal to head left.

"Like hell."

He shot her a sharp look.

"You'll lose time." She didn't want to increase his worry by adding that he might need her medical expertise when he found his cousin's son.

"I don't like the idea—"

This time she didn't hesitate to put her hand on his forearm. "I came here to help, Jesse," she said softly.

He looked at her. She imagined he was unaware of the rare warmth that shone in his eyes.

"So, can the arguments, cowboy."

The warmth in his eyes flickered with amusement before he remembered himself and made his features a mask once again. Many men hid their emotions. But was Jesse hiding more? Amy wondered.

Jesse knew that trained Red Cross volunteers, along with Flo Templeton and volunteers from the ladies' auxiliaries, were manning the high school and more than capable of handling anything that might arise before the storm hit. Any serious emergencies requiring Amy's more extensive skills were likely to occur after the hurricane. If anything had happened to Michael and his friends, timing could be critical. They would need Amy now. Still, if she were in the evacuation center, she would be safe. And so would he, separated from her inquiring gaze and pointed questions.

Jesse radioed the dispatcher at the rescue station. "Any reports from the coastal patrol? Teenage boys picked up on their way to catch a big wave?"

"Not that I know of. What's up?"

"My cousin Clare's boy, Michael, and a few of his buddies decided to head down along the shore to hang ten on the high waves coming in from the storm."

"Can't imagine how they got there. The interstate south is closed to everything except police and emergency vehicles."

"They could have taken the back route. It's longer but they would have avoided any barriers."

"I'll send out a BOLO, see if anyone knows anything, although communication has been hit and miss."

"Let me know if any reports come through. I'm heading down there now. Dr. Sherwood is going with me. If Clare calls, tell her not to worry. I'll find the boys and bring them home. Any other problems?"

"The usual scramble for supplies, long lines, short nerves, but otherwise, things have been relatively quiet, knock on wood. Not much to do now but wait."

Jesse looked at the sky with its pale-green cast and the rains like a river. He held tight as the winds rocked the Bronco. He glanced at his passenger. She was also looking into the storm's strange light. *Wait,* he thought. *Until all hell breaks loose.*

"A BOLO?" Amy questioned.

"Be on the lookout," Jesse answered.

"Right." Amy peered through the window, saw the rains pelting the grass flat. The farm lagoons had been drained to their lowest level, the pastures emptied, livestock herded into shelter. The blinding rain and battering wind slowed the Bronco's progress. The radio had been reduced to bursts of static until, with a frustrated sigh, Jesse snapped it off.

State police vehicles blocked the on ramp to the interstate heading south. Jesse eased the vehicle over to the shoulder and jumped out into the rain and wind toward one of the cruisers. Amy's professional eye saw a pronounced leaning toward the left in his first steps, but it was quickly corrected. The wet, the rain, the wind would aggravate old wounds, make them ache like a newly broken heart.

Jesse climbed back into the cab a few minutes later, bringing the wind and a new dampness inside. The police cruiser pulled over onto the ramp's shoulder, allowing the Bronco access.

"Communication's sporadic due to the heavy winds and rains. If the leading bands of the storm move on and he can get a signal, he'll radio the other patrols along the coast to see if any teenage boys were found."

"Michael and his friends are probably headed home as we speak," Amy said, "bragging to each other all the way."

It was silent inside the cab for a few minutes, then Jesse muttered, "God willing."

Amy brushed at a smear of dirt on her slacks. She'd brought several changes of clothes, all permanent press and designed to coordinate. She was a sensible person. Even as a teenager, she'd been focused and determined. Miss Goody Two-shoes, the meaner kids would say. But they'd been right. She'd never done anything wild in her life...until she fell in love with Jesse Boone.

She looked at the man beside her with the same name. A less sensible woman would say it was fate, not coincidence, that had brought them together. Despite all logical objections, a less sensible woman would have believed the boy she had loved fourteen years ago sat beside her now as a man. A less sensible woman would have wasted precious time searching for a possibility that didn't exist.

She was not that woman.

"How old is the boy?"

"Turned sixteen a month ago. He doesn't even have his damn driver's license yet."

"Sixteen." Amy repeated. A lifetime ago. She studied Jesse's grim profile. "What an age. Not only do you think you know everything, you truly believe you're invulnerable. Later you look back and realize how truly stupid you were."

He glanced at her. She knew what he saw. She looked down at her unpolished chipped nails and experienced a rare yearning for color, if only a pale-pink tint. She would like to say her sensible shoes, trim chinos and button-down shirt were chosen for their utility. She would even like to imagine that beneath her conservative outfit were silk panties and a low-cut lace camisole instead of one hundred percent white cotton briefs and a no-frills, functional bra. But it would not be the truth. She used the excuse she was too busy to bother with the extras that were a part of other women's daily routine—makeup, any hairstyle more complicated than a twist into a barrette, shoes with heels, gold chains that sparkled.

"Sorry, Doc, you don't strike me as ever having been the stupid type."

Once, she thought. She surprised herself with a smile as the memory came with a strength equal to the elements shuddering their vehicle now. *Once, when she fell in love with a wild, dark-eyed boy.*

Jesse caught her smile. She'd seen surprise on his face also. That face so unfamiliar, yet there was something in those eyes. Those dark eyes. Her smile dissolved. Once she'd been the stupid type. No more.

"You'd be wrong, Sheriff. I've had my share of foolish moments, although I'll admit, they were many moons ago and few and far between."

"Don't know anyone who goes through life without a mistake or two."

"My aunt says, 'Make a mistake once and you're human. Make it twice and you're a fool.'"

"Is that what you did? Learn from your mistakes?"

She looked him square in the face. "The lesson of a lifetime."

Silence filled the cab.

"How about you?" Amy asked.

He glanced at her.

"No mistakes?" She had no right, but something urged her on.

His mouth formed a tight, wry smile, twisting the thin scar along his jaw line. "No one gets thirty-two years under their belt without mistakes."

Thirty-two. Same age as herself. Same age as the Jesse Boone she'd known. She stared at him, hearing the pummeling wind and rain outside, the pounding of her heart within. He ignored her stare, but she saw the tension turn up a notch in his strong, sober features. She reached out her hand, trained to heal. She had no right.

She didn't care.

She touched his forearm. The skin was still damp but the flesh was warm, hard muscle underneath. He lowered his gaze, his face a cool mask.

"This." Her fingers moved, lightly traced a scar. "How did this mistake happen?"

CHAPTER FOUR

HE JERKED his arm away. He stared straight ahead into the storm. Anger burned in his eyes. She had touched something much deeper. She did not rationalize her question with professional license, the insensitivity that came from the assembly line of illness and injury that made up a doctor's day. She had a personal reason for asking about this man's private past. An irrational need warring within her that forced her blunt questions. She was ashamed of herself.

"Look..." she began to apologize.

"It was an accident." His interruption surprised her.

Let it be. She turned to the man beside her but found she couldn't let it go. "An automobile accident?"

He shot a warning glance at her.

"None of my damn business, Sheriff?"

He nodded.

"You're right." But she didn't apologize. She sat silent for a few heartbeats, telling herself she was out of line.

"Industrial? Agricultural?"

He glared at her for a second, then began to slowly shake his head from side to side. The anger in his features tempered. To her own astonishment, his mouth quirked into a half smile. Still shaking his head, he turned his attention back to the highway. "You don't give up, do you?"

She scanned his body, now healed from what must have been a beating. "Obviously, neither do you."

He drove another quarter mile. He did not look at her when he said, "It was a long time ago." He turned his head. Their eyes met. "It's over."

Except for the scars that were more than physical. Amy had seen the devastation a serious accident could cause. Lives that had been happy, healthy, whole were consumed by the sheer terror of possibly never taking a step again without assistance, never speaking without slurring, never waking without an ache somewhere to remind the victims of the mere seconds that had changed their life forever.

"Jess." She said the name without realizing it until she heard its soft reverberations. Every feature on his face held firm. He did not look at her.

She had no right. Except she had once loved a boy named Jesse Boone. Now, beside her, was a man with the same name, the same age. What if he was the Jesse Boone who'd disappeared from her life without warning? What then? Would an explanation erase the pain of fourteen years?

She looked at the man, looked for the boy she'd loved so fiercely. She had to be certain. "What happened?"

Jesse silently cursed her. Her stubbornness, her persistence had not lessened. On the contrary, her determination had only intensified in fourteen years. It was these cornerstones of Amy's character that had brought her mother to his bedside after the accident. The woman, bespectacled, bowed at the shoulders from years of working in the canning plant and raising a daughter who had been given every opportunity she herself had not been privilege to, had sat at his bedside and pleaded.

A full scholarship, son. Amy's mother had looked at him through glasses that dominated her thin face, her eyes the same blue-green as her daughter's, magnified by the lenses. She'd taken his hand. He had barely felt the grip, but the veins along the top of her hand had stood out in anxious relief.

You know my daughter, Jesse. She learns of this... Her glance had swept his body, now bandaged and wired, fed by tubes, monitored by machines. *And she won't go. She'll give up the scholarship, everything she's worked so hard for.* Both her hands had clasped his. *Don't do that to her. Don't take her dream from her.*

He'd known she'd been right. The fact did nothing to lessen the pain that was a thousand time more wretched than any physical injuries. Amy would have rushed to his side and stayed there. At the minimum, it would have been years of operations and therapy, surgery to fuse the bones, rebuild the shattered jaw. Even so, the doctors hadn't been able to guarantee that his body, once that of a promising athlete, would ever be able to take a small step unsupported.

He had not been able to speak that day. The shattered bones in his face had been wired tight. He had not even been able to squeeze the hands clinging to his in utter desperation. Using every once of strength not already sucked from his body, he'd nodded. It was all he could give Amy's mother. He saw from the relief and gratitude in her face that it was enough.

Thank you. Thank you. She'd stood and leaned over to kiss his bandaged brow. *You're doing the right thing.*

He looked at Amy now, his selfish need to tell her the truth warring again with his need to do the right thing. *Let it be, Jess,* he told himself, unconsciously using the name she'd so often softly spoken fourteen years ago. *I love you, Jess.* He still heard those words—whispered in a young girl's voice, at night in the darkness. *Let it be,* he told himself again. *Let it remain in the darkness.*

His gaze went hard on her, his annoyance evident.

She smiled back at him, telling him he didn't frighten her none. Not that he had expected to. Some things had changed over the past years, but some things were eternal. One was the woman's grit.

"None of your damn business," he answered with a hard edge of warning in his voice. He snapped the radio back on. It crackled, kept breaking up, the distance and high winds interfering with the reception. He fiddled with the tuner, hoping for a clear signal. Snippets of reports interrupted by static came through. He turned up the volume. "Landfall farther southwest… unexpected wind patterns…the Gulf… less-populated along Mexican border."

"Sounds like it's turning, breaking up." Jesse could almost hear the men seated on the diner stools telling one another, 'Just as I predicted.' He looked over at Amy. He was far from being out of danger himself.

"Your cousin's son and his friends may have lucked out this time," Amy said.

"Maybe from the hurricane."

"But Michael will have to deal with you?"

"And his mother."

"Seems to me, your cousin and her boys are lucky to have you around."

He shrugged. "I help out when I can. It's hard enough being teenagers. Add to the fact their father takes off with a woman not much older than they are, and you have a set up for big-time trouble."

"It's hard for teenagers not having a parent around."

Silently Jesse agreed. He had never known his own mother. His father had had many faults, but he'd never abandoned his son, which was exactly why Jesse had been unable to abandon him when he'd wakened Jesse in the middle of the night six months before the accident and said, "Come on, boy, we're moving on." No, his father had never left his son behind. Until death.

He glanced at Amy, saw her thoughtful expression and wondered if she was remembering her own adolescence as the child of a single parent. The experience had provided a common bond that had drawn them closer. He'd never talked about the pain of not knowing a parent with anyone before Amy. Nor had she. Although her mother had tried to make up for the lack, Amy had suffered from not knowing her father. She had sworn she would never raise a child in a single-parent household. She would never have a child until she was certain she could give it a loving home with both a mother and a father. He'd sworn the same. Funny thing was, when they'd made the promise, they'd believed it would be the two of them raising children born of their love and happiness.

A gust of wind came up strong, snapping him out of the past. The wheel tried to pull hard to the right, but Jesse held steady, focusing past the windshield wipers beating furiously, to the stretch of highway ahead. He had gotten through the past fourteen years. Now all he had to do was get through the next two, three, four days at the most.

Amy could smell the sea as they came closer to the coast. They headed into open territory, the sheltering illusion of being inland gone. The wind, unencumbered, sped freely over the expanse of water and sky, bending the crowns of the scattered palms. She felt the wind's push, bowing the vehicle's side, sucking in around the edges as if it wanted them gone. Yet this whip of a wind was only a mild messenger of what the storm's wrath could be.

Jesse continued to check the radio, hoping to make contact to learn if the boys had been found. He moved between channels but the storm was too strong. Communication had been knocked out.

Amy saw concern and frustration etching lines into Jesse's face. This man would be a good father, she thought. "I'll bet your cousin's boy and his friends are riding into Turning Point right now. If not, we'll find them. We won't go back until we do or we're sure they're not here."

Jesse stared out at the rain falling like a sea, sweeping in horizontally. "It'll take us an hour to check all along the shore—maybe longer with these driving conditions."

"From those last reports, it sounds like the storm might miss the Texas coast completely."

Jesse scanned the darkening sky, although nightfall was hours away.

"We've come this far, Sheriff."

Jesse looked at the woman beside him and fell in love all over again.

"You shouldn't have come." His voice was gruff.

"It was my choice."

"Foolish one," he said, trying to offset the feelings inside him.

She smiled, as if amused by him. She'd always been the smart one of the two of them. "Not my first and probably won't be my last."

The wind shook the vehicle with renewed vehemence. Jesse's brow pulled low with worry. If those reports were wrong… If Michael and his friends were still out at the beach… He pressed the accelerator. Five miles an hour faster was all he dared. They drove parallel to the shore. The sea rose with a siren's scream, waves eighteen feet high moving in fast, churning the water white with wide, breaking sprays.

The teenagers' trip was a dangerous venture. Yet Amy could understand why they were tempted. She thought of her own son at home. Amy had lived in Courage Bay with Aunt Betts, her mother's older unmarried sister, from the time she'd gone to medical college. Her aunt had helped care for Ian since his birth, and would keep a stern eye on him. Ian was also younger than these boys. Yet not many years from now, Amy herself could be the one anxiously waiting for a phone to ring with the news her son was safe from a dangerous escapade. She didn't realize she'd sighed aloud until she saw Jesse glance over at her.

"Problem?" he asked her, one brow lifted in inquiry.

She shook her head, declining to explain. She could have secrets too.

They passed a motel, three-quarters surrounded by a stucco half wall. A wooden sign inscribed Dolphin Inn swung madly. A middle-aged man hammered plywood across a window beneath the building's overhang. He stopped and turned as he heard the vehicle approach.

Jesse pulled into the drive. "I'm going to check to see if he's seen a bunch of teenagers riding by. I'll be right back." He jumped out of the Bronco and sprinted across the drive.

The rain pelted the windshield. If the boys were down here, Amy doubted they were still surfing. The winds were too high, the waves so powerful that even the most experienced surfers would risk injury. She scanned the shore, trying to see past the storm for something, anything that would lead them to the boys. She saw Jesse point toward the boardwalk. He had removed his hat so he wouldn't lose it. The wind swept his hair away from his forehead, exposing a clean profile, an intense, grim gaze. The man shook his head. They spoke a few seconds more. Again the man shook his head. Jesse offered his hand before leaving. He clasped the man on the shoulder as they shook.

When he came back into the van, he smelled of rain and wind and dampness. His shirt clung to his chest, outlining firm muscle that must have taken years of intense, painful workouts to restore after his obviously serious accident. She stared at his chest and found herself wondering how long it had taken for medical science and sheer will to put this man back together.

He turned and reached in the back for his hat. He pushed back his damp, dark hair, made even blacker by the rain, before he settled the hat on his head, shadowing his features and whatever emotions they might expose.

"Did he see anything?"

"Said he saw a car with surfboards on the roof earlier today. It was headed in the direction of the point."

"Did he see the boys come back through?"

"No, but he says that doesn't mean they didn't. He was in and out all afternoon, boarding up the motel. The boys could easily have passed by again without him seeing them." Jesse turned the vehicle toward the Point.

"Has the man heard any recent reports on the storm?"

Jesse shook his head. "Storm took electricity out about an hour ago. Last the man heard, the storm was still heading north, past Corpus Christi."

"The reports we heard sounded as if it had weakened, turned south."

"Without radio contact, it's hard to know."

Amy looked over her shoulder and saw the man wave to them as they pulled away. "I'm surprised he's still here."

"He's not planning on going anywhere. Tried to talk him into heading up to Turning Point. Told him about the shelter at the school, but he wouldn't hear of it. Said he'd never left yet, and he wasn't about to start. Said the beach was his home. He's seen four hurricanes already and lived to tell about them. Said he and a few others even had a party the night Hurricane Harriet rolled in."

"Foolishness obviously doesn't end with the teenage years," Amy noted.

"Amen." Jesse watched the road, scanning the surroundings as he drove. Amy did the same. "He's probably not the only one down here who ignored the evacuation order. He said there's a drive-in a few miles south on the bay that generally remains open for the residents who stay behind and the plain curious who sneak in to see the storm. The boys might have stopped there to get something to eat."

Most of the buildings they passed were boarded with plywood. The houses on the beach stood on stilts, towering optimistically above the sea's surge. Decks had been cleared, but the odd wicker chaise and bamboo rocker flew by, thrown about by the wind. The trees bent low, threatening to break.

They came to the drive-in. The neon lights trimming its flat roof were dark. As the man had predicted, several vehicles were parked in the lot. The picnic tables were chained, their umbrellas removed. A half dozen people clustered under the drive-in's overhang, facing the sea, sharing a twelve-pack of beer. They turned toward the Bronco as Jesse pulled into the lot. Their gazes narrowed as they noted the sheriff's star on the vehicle's door. This time Amy followed Jesse. He shot her a look as she stepped outside but didn't try to stop her. Heads nodded in response to Jesse's greeting but expressions remained cautious.

"I'm looking for a group of teenage boys," Jesse told them. "Came down here to surf on the big waves brought in by the storm. I was hoping they stopped here or one of you saw them."

Everyone seemed to relax. "Ask Marnie," one man said, cocking his head toward the drive-in window. Others nodded. "If they stopped for food, she would have served them."

Jesse went to the wide window where orders were placed. A heavyset woman was packing supplies into cupboards.

"Ma'am?" Jesse said at the window.

"No orders," she barked, her back to the window. "Electricity's been out and the generator's almost out of juice. I'm packing up and heading inland myself." She turned, took in Jesse's uniform.

Jesse touched the brim of his hat. "Sheriff Jesse Boone, ma'am. Come down from Turning Point."

"Sorry, Sheriff." Wiping her hands on a towel, she came toward the window. "What can I do for you?"

"We're looking for a group of teenage boys might have passed through here. They were heading to the shore to surf the big waves brought in by the storm."

"Never fails." The woman folded her towel, set it on a cardboard box. "Get a group of young yahoos every time, wanting to prove themselves by downing a case of beer and riding the waves. I don't know who's worse—them or the ones who head here and order hot fudge sundaes as if it were a Sunday outing." The woman looked out at the group, her expression resigned.

Her gaze returned to Jesse and Amy. "A group of boys did come by, but it was earlier, after lunch. I'd say one, one-thirty. They ordered burgers, onion rings, milkshakes to go. They were keen to get on their way. There were four of them, I think. They had their surfboards strapped to the car."

"You hear them say where they were heading?"

The woman shook her head. "They drove off south. Probably heading for Padre Point. That'd be my guess. Popular spot with the young set."

"How far off is it?"

"About ten miles."

"And you didn't see them come back through?"

"They didn't stop here if they did. But that's not to say they didn't ride a few big ones, have their fun and head home."

Jesse glanced at the group gathered under the overhang. "What about these people?"

She shrugged. "There's always a few who come out, thinking it's fun and games. Damn fools."

"What about you?"

"I'm heading to my sister's in Three Rivers soon as I close up here."

"Might want to make that soon."

"As soon as I shut down the generator, I'm on my way."

"Glad to hear it." Jesse touched the brim of his hat again. "Thanks for your help."

"Wish it was more," the woman told them both.

Jesse and Amy moved away from the window, back to the group. "There's an evacuation center set up at the Turning Point high school."

"Last report said the storm shifted to the southwest," an elderly man said. "We'll see the wind and the rain, but down by the Mexican border will get the brunt of it."

"That report was a while ago. Anything could have happened since communication went down. Even if the storm did turn, you'd be safer on higher ground."

"Thanks, Sheriff. Good to know if things get too wild round here."

"It'll be too late by then."

The older man, his face narrow and cheeks sunken by age, took a long pull on his beer. "Then I'll be here to meet it."

"Damn fool." Jesse echoed the drive-in owner's declaration beneath his breath. To the group, he said, "If any of you change your mind, we'll be coming back through here after we check out the point. You can follow us or there's room in the back if you want a ride."

"Thanks, Sheriff, but if things start to get too wild, we'll head to Hank's house. Sixteen feet above ground, it's plenty high enough not to worry about being washed away should the tidal surge hit."

"What are you going to do when the winds rip the roof off?"

"We'll be fine, Sheriff. Come on back down after this thing passes through. Bring the pretty lady and we'll all have a beer together and raise our bottles to Damon."

"If I do, I expect you all to be here."

"It's a promise, Sheriff."

Amy and Jesse headed back to the Bronco. Jesse took a final look at the group as he started the engine. Several waved. He released a frustrated sigh.

"Crazy old goats," Amy said with such vehement disgust that Jesse half smiled as he steered into the storm. "Drinking beer and sitting around swapping fish stories as if this were no more than a Friday-night poker game. I hope they get the damn pants scared off them when the storm hits."

"If it does hit, they'll lose more than their pants."

"Couldn't you arrest them? Force them to take shelter?"

"Technically, they aren't breaking any laws."

"We should have strung them up like rodeo bulls, thrown them in the back of the Bronco and hauled their stubborn butts back to Turning Point."

Jesse's smiled widened against his wishes. "They're men, not livestock."

"Well, a rock's got more common sense than the lot of them."

"Maybe, but I've lived long enough in Turning Point to know when a man's mind is made up, there's little chance of changing it."

Amy crossed her arms over her chest and huffed an indignant breath. "Sometimes stubborn is another word for plain pigheaded."

He turned his face away, hiding the smile he'd concealed several times already. She'd been as fervent and fiery at eighteen, her passion no small part of her appeal. He'd had no doubt when she'd come to tutor him that she saw him as a quest, a confirmation of her fervent belief that any human being with enough grit and guts could accomplish anything. What he hadn't realized was that she would make him believe it too. She would have sacrificed her dream for him. It was why he'd sacrificed his.

Jesse examined the sky again. Amy followed his gaze.

"There's time," she told him.

But neither knew how much.

CHAPTER FIVE

AMY ALLOWED five minutes of silence before she began questioning Jesse again. His attempts to avoid answering her earlier questions had only increased her curiosity. She was determined to learn as much as she could about the sheriff.

"So, you never married?" she asked point-blank.

He gave her a long, level look.

"You didn't think I was going to let you off the hook that easy?" She smiled. He didn't.

"According to Lurie, you're the catch of the county and the ladies are willing to wait in line for their turn."

Jesse frowned, vertical lines forming between his brow. "I warned you not to put much stock in Lurie's tales. She's a great gal, but what comes from between those lips tends to be embellished, if you know what I mean."

"She said you're harder to hogtie than a prize-winning bull, but you let the ladies know that up front. A real gentleman. Only that makes them try all the harder."

Jesse shook his head. Then, as if in surrender, he released a low chuckle. Amy smiled despite her realization he was charming her as easily as he had the female population of the lower Texas quadrant.

"Lurie thinks once you find the right girl, you'll fall faster than a twenty-one-year-old at his first happy hour."

"For once Lurie is right."

Amy was surprised by his rare frankness. Encouraged, she continued. "You're not afraid of commitment. You just haven't found the right girl yet?"

"I didn't say I hadn't found the right girl yet." He stopped as if realizing where the conversation was heading. "Are you always so damn nosy?"

"No," she said, so self-righteously a smile pulled at the corners of his mouth. He caught himself and continued scowling. However, she'd glimpsed the good-natured man beneath the frown. She suspected the sheriff was deliberately putting on an alternative face for her. She intended to find out the reason.

"Why the twenty questions?"

She ignored his question to ask one of her own. "So you found the right girl?"

He kept his attention on the highway, ignoring her.

"You did find the right girl but you didn't realize it at the time?"

He gave a long sigh. She had decided he wasn't going to answer, when he stared out into the fierce storm and said, "I realized it."

His features seemed to give way and his strong face, handsome even in its scowling mask, filled with pain. As quick as it came, it was gone.

"What happened?" she said in almost a whisper.

"She was married," he said without looking at her.

"And..." Amy hesitated. He glanced at her as if waiting. "There's never been anyone else?"

"No," he stated.

"You will never marry?"

Pain flickered across his features again. "It would be cruel to marry one woman when I loved another."

"Did she love you?"

His voice softened. "She did."

"Did she know you loved her?"

The smallest smile curved his mouth. "She did."

"But she married someone else?"

The smile faded. "It wasn't her fault."

"Do you ever see her?"

He turned and looked at her. "Yes."

"Is she happy?"

Their eyes met. "Yes," he said. "She is." He smiled as if the woman's happiness was his.

Amy studied the man beside her. Several seconds of silence passed. "I'm sorry," she told him.

He looked at her again, smiled softly. "It wasn't your fault."

They drove in silence. They were almost to their destination when Amy said, "I was married once, but it didn't work out."

"Jesus." For the first time, the wind won. The Bronco swerved toward the road's shoulder. Jesse's arm shot out protectively across Amy. His other hand regained control of the vehicle and eased it back onto the highway.

Her simple statement had hit him like a shot to the

chest. His heart hammered against his ribs. The storm surged around them. The winds shrieked. The sky darkened in warning. *Don't hope, Jesse.*

He waited until he was certain his voice wouldn't reveal him. "We must almost be at Padre Point."

She smiled. "I'm not worried, Sheriff."

He waited another minute before he could ask, "So, you're divorced?"

"About four years now."

His heart turned over. *Four years.* He kept his tone mildly interested. "What happened?"

She glanced at him as if surprised by his interest.

"Malcolm was a good man. Older than me, but then again, I've always been mature for my age."

She threw in a wry smile that Jesse could not return. *Four years,* he thought.

"He was a professor."

Jesse raised a brow.

She mocked his expression. "Don't be shocked, Sheriff. He was only thirty-eight when we met."

"How old were you?"

"Twenty-four."

Jesse raised his other brow, causing her smile to widen.

"It wasn't easy from the first. My friends found him dry and boring. I thought his friends pompous. But Malcolm represented everything I one day hoped to be—settled, established and successful in his career. And wise. Bottom-line, he was stable. And stable was everything I desired."

Why? Jesse asked silently. Because it was safer than

having your heart shattered by an insensitive teenager who had promised you the world and then disappeared. His own heart, which he had kept under lock and key for so long, contracted, confirming what he had feared when he'd stepped into the firehouse and set eyes on Amy. The heart he'd held still for so long had begun to beat again.

"Malcolm had lost his wife several years earlier to pancreatic cancer. He was kind and tragic. I was a struggling student, very serious. I was fortunate to have the support of my family, especially my aunt, who I lived with at the time, but..."

Her eyes turned vague, and a flatness had come into her voice. For a moment, Jesse feared she wouldn't continue.

"We were both lonely, Malcolm and I. We respected and cared about each other, but loneliness is not a good foundation for a lifetime together. We thought we could give each other what we both craved."

She stared out into the storm as if seeing her own past. "We were wrong," she finished simply.

"How long were you married?"

"Let's see." She thought. "We married over the semester midwinter break in February. I was in my fourth year of medical school. I was twenty-five."

They had just been newlyweds, Jesse realized. It had been more than seven years and countless operations before he had been strong enough to look for Amy. And after three months of searching, he'd finally found her. He'd called her telephone number in Courage Bay,

California, his heart slamming wildly with each ring. Her husband had answered.

That had been March seven years ago. What if he had called a month, six weeks earlier?

"Three years later, it was over," Amy continued. "But it was an amicable divorce. Actually we're still really good friends. He often comes and spends holidays with Ian and me."

Jesse's heart bottomed out. Amy had been divorced four years. She was a beautiful, smart, successful woman. Of course she'd be involved with someone else. Still, spending the holidays with your ex-husband and your new lover sounded a little too contemporary…even for California.

Perhaps the new relationship wasn't that serious. *Don't hope,* he told himself. But it had been hope that had driven him through the first seven years after the accident and played a large role in his remarkable recovery. The hope of being well enough, strong enough again to be the man Amy could love.

"And many times, Malcolm and Ian make plans and spend the whole weekend together. They're both die-hard Dodgers fans, while I'm afraid what I know about baseball could fit on the head of a pin."

Jesse raised his brows. "Your ex-husband and your new boyfriend go to baseball games together?"

Amy released a sweet, soft laugh that made his blood hum. "Ian's my son."

Her son. Jesse's hope spiked. Tiny shells and small pebbles being swept up by the wind clattered against the sides of the van as if echoing the confusion of emotions inside him. Maybe it wasn't sheer coincidence that brought her to Turning Point. Maybe…

Don't hope, Jesse.

He looked at the woman beside him. Too late.

"So, you aren't involved with anyone now?"

"Are you always so damn nosy, Sheriff?" She pretended indignation, but her eyes twinkled like stardust.

"No."

She looked out at the storm. Her smile disappeared. "No, I'm not involved with anyone. I learned my lesson."

"What lesson was that?" He downshifted to maneuver a curve.

"Life doesn't give you second chances."

He had to tell her she was wrong. He had to tell her everything. When he had believed she was still married, he had feared the truth would have only served his own selfish needs and caused her pain and confusion. But now… His hand rested on the gear shift, close enough to take her hand in his. He opened his fingers.

"Jesse?"

He heard his name on her lips as if it were a dream. But her face was turned away to the window. She peered into the gray-green of the storm to the east. "Do you see something over there?"

He shifted his gaze the same direction as hers. A flash of red cut through the rain-whipped landscape. Slowing down, he steered toward the road's shoulder to take a closer look. A large, long form was pressed flat against a tree. He peered into the vast gray scape, the rain making everything a blur. The wind took the object and tossed it easily. On the object's underbelly, Jesse saw the design of red and blue flames.

"It's Michael's surfboard. What's left of it." At least a third of the board was missing. He scanned the area.

"The wind must have ripped it off the car's roof," Amy said.

He made no comment, slowly easing the van back onto the road, searching for a sign of the boy or his friends. The wind pummeled the van, forcing it back toward the shoulder. Jesse struggled to control the vehicle as it veered. Spitting gravel joined the shells and pebbles clattering against the sides. The winds were too high, too strong. They passed a small marker. Padre Point. One Mile.

"We're almost there," Amy said with an encouraging smile. Neither commented on the increasing fury outside. The rain continued to fall, and the van's headlights shone into the grayness. Beach houses clustered several hundred yards back from the shore. As the van rounded a curve, almost to their destination, Jesse saw a small, weathered A-frame building with a faded painted sign proclaiming The Sea Shack. Two hundred yards away the flat land formed a point and disappeared into the sea. Waves rose and fell violently, colliding with each other. Above, a thickening bank of clouds merged into a dark gray wall. Jesse parked at the sand's edge, the van's headlights slicing through the gloom. Pieces of a surfboard, blue and red, lay scattered on the sand until the wind caught them and carried them several yards. Otherwise the beach was deserted.

Jesse reached for the door handle. "I'm going to take a closer look."

Amy reached for her door handle.

"Stay here."

The expression on his face stopped her from arguing. She let go of the door handle and watched Jesse, the rain and sand and shells pelting his body. He leaned into the wind as he made his way to the shoreline. She watched him several seconds, then a movement in the side mirror caught her attention. A cloud was coming from the same direction they'd just traveled. It hung low, sliding across the flat length of the beach, black and purple and darker than the sky that surrounded it. At first, she thought it an illusion, the blurred images of water, sky and storm playing tricks with her vision, fueling her imagination like a child seeing ghouls in the night's shadows. She shifted to see the low, flying saucer shape stand on its end, reaching out a long finger to skim the beach. She leapt out of the van and ran toward the shore where Jesse stood. He turned as she screamed his name, catching her as she stumbled, and drew her to the hard solid wall of his chest.

"What the—?" His arms automatically circled around her and she stayed in his embrace as she pointed out the long-fingered shape. It touched down and pulled up, as if determining if it was in the right place, then suddenly detached from the cloud, driven by a life of its own.

They stood watching it for a moment, fascinated as the shape wobbled back and forth across the flat shore as if trying to decide which way to go. Not until it veered right, toward where they stood, did they move. Jesse's arms still embracing her, Amy ran with him toward the A-frame two hundred yards from the shore. She glanced over her shoulder once, saw the long, spiny shape move up, touch down. They made it to the building, the world black around them. Jesse broke down the door and pulled Amy in. She swung around for one last look, saw a tree snap like a stick, felt the ground beneath the building tremble, then the building itself, the windows rattling in their frames. Jesse pulled her with him toward a door, looking for a crawlspace, but the building had been built on a slab.

"Lie down," he yelled.

She did as he said, her body flat against the sand and grit that covered the floor. He arched over her, his body a breath from hers. She closed her eyes, the earth's tremor moving through her. She listened to the sounds of things cracking and falling outside. She felt the wild thump of her own heart and that of the heart above her. Outside, the world roared like a creature in pain, its anguish eternal.

And then as swiftly as it had started, it was over. The world went still, the silence even greater after the fury. The only trembling was Amy's involuntary shaking. Above her, Jesse shifted, rolled away from her. He laid a tentative hand on her shoulder and bent close.

"Amy? Are you okay?"

His breath whispered against her cheek, the concern in his voice thick. She tried to still the trembling, but her body would not cooperate. "I'm fine," she said in a quivering voice.

"It's moved on. It's over for now." He stayed close

to her, his warmth welcome. She turned her head to find him. His mouth, a mere inch from hers, took in a swift breath.

"I'm fine," she whispered.

He looked deeply into her eyes as if to determine the truth. Her past seemed to rise like the storm outside. Two people locked in a vortex of emotion, communicating without speaking. Her shaking did not subside. The face was different, but the eyes, the emotion were familiar. "Jess?"

He pulled back as if struck a blow. His eyes went flat, and he schooled his features into their familiar mask. She pushed herself up to a sitting position, her gaze still not releasing him. He stood and offered her his hand. She wrapped her fingers around his, and something as fierce as the power they'd just witnessed ignited between them.

Once she was on her feet and steady, he let her go. He crossed to the windows. She followed him, brushing off the sand and sawdust clinging to her wet clothes.

The tornado had cut a random path of destruction. It had missed the building where Jesse and Amy sought shelter, but a tree ten feet away had been ripped up by its roots. If it had fallen in the opposite direction, it would have sliced the building right down the middle.

She heard Jesse swear and saw the source of his distress. The Bronco's front end lay beneath a fallen tree, its windshield smashed, the top of the roof flattened.

"Looks like we're stuck here for a little while. Until communication is restored. There's no way we can look for the boys in this. Fortunately we've got shelter." He studied the sky. "Tornado must have spun off from the storm. Onshore tornadoes often sprout from the outer rain bands."

"Do you think that's the end of it?"

He lowered his gaze to Amy. She saw his hand rise as if to brush her cheek. "God willing." He turned away, not touching her. "More likely than not, that's it. The storm must have continued southwest, a tornado or two breaking off to the north. The heavy rains and high winds will probably continue and result in inland flooding, but that may be the worst of it." He moved toward the door. "The tree missed the back of the Bronco. I'll go...get some supplies."

Amy followed him.

"I can handle it."

"I don't doubt that," she said.

When she continued to the doorway, he placed a hand on her arm to stop her.

"You'll be safer inside."

That remained to be seen, she thought as she felt the heat of his palm against her flesh, the hum between them.

"Stay here." He stepped outside.

"Like hell." She followed him into the storm. The earth had lost its trembling fury, but the wind and the rain had not gentled. On the contrary, as if inspired by the force that had just passed, their power seemed to have heightened.

Jesse swung up the Bronco's rear door. Leaning in, he pulled out a box and handed it to Amy.

"It's light," she yelled above the wind and rain. "Pile some things on top of it."

He added a plastic bag of items. "Go, I'll get the rest."

She easily ran the distance back to the building even with the additional weight. She vowed never to curse her daily three-mile run again. Jesse followed behind her and set another box and her medical bag on the long counter that ran the length of the building's front room, which must have served as a dining room.

"Is there more?" Amy asked as she released her barrette. She pushed back the damp tendrils from her forehead and finger-combed her hair before twisting it up once more and refastening the barrette. She swung her gaze and caught Jesse watching her, his eyes dark. She blamed their intensity on the shadowy light.

He swallowed, the muscles of his throat working. "Some bottled water, blankets, pillows." A huskiness came into his voice as if his throat were dry. He swallowed again.

"There's food, a portable light." He indicated the box he'd brought in. "I'll go get the last few things out of the Bronco."

She watched him go, then turned her attention away from the man who had mystified her since he'd stepped into the firehouse this morning. As she moved toward the boxes, she inspected the temporary shelter. The building was not large but wide at the bottom, narrowing to a peak at the top. An open banister revealed a loft, where people must have sat to enjoy the view of the sea. The building looked long-unoccupied but at one time probably had served as a small restaurant. A few tables and chairs and three counter stools were stacked along one wall. A swinging door on the other side of the counter opened to a narrow kitchen with shelves and cupboards and wide gaps along the wall where commercial appliances once stood. She moved into the cooking area, opened a cupboard or two, a drawer here and there. Her search revealed an assortment of utensils, odd cups and plates, a half bottle of vinegar and the unmistakable droppings of mice. A heavy door revealed a walk-in storage room off the kitchen, its generous shelves empty except for an opened roll of paper towels and an industrial-size plastic jar of mayonnaise.

She went back into the main room and opened the boxes. Inside the first she found peanut butter, crackers, a can of nuts, a can of juice, paper cups and plates, plastic silverware and napkins. Beneath the paper supplies was a bag of cookies and a box of pink-and-white candy-coated licorice known as Good & Plenty.

She pulled out the box. As a teenager, she had never sat through a movie without devouring a king-sized box of the candy. Jesse had teased her about her addiction.

The door opened, announcing Jesse's return with a blast of rain and wind. He set down the last of the supplies, stripped off his rain gear, and removed his hat. Water puddled about him. Outside, broken limbs slapped the building.

"There's an electric line down not far from here. It was snapping like a hungry gator, but it should go dead soon.

The power grids today have a programmed safety feature that kicks in during a disaster, shutting down everything."

It was seven o'clock. The weather forecasters had originally predicted if it did hit, Hurricane Damon would make landfall around midnight.

Amy faced Jesse, still holding the candy in her hands. Another coincidence? She had five hours to find out. She didn't realize she was shaking until she heard the candy rattling against the box.

Five hours to learn the truth.

CHAPTER SIX

JESSE LOOKED at the Good & Plenty box in Amy's hands and knew he'd made a mistake. "That's my part-time clerk's idea of survival food."

"I've never gotten through a double feature without a box." Amy watched Jesse's face.

He avoided her gaze, instead inspecting their surroundings as she had done. "Myself, I'm a Mallomar man, but I doubt my clerk had the foresight to pack any of those." He bent toward the box and lifted out a large portable light and a smaller flashlight.

"The Jesse Boone I knew, the one I was talking about earlier, now he liked jelly doughnuts. Would eat a dozen and a half of them for breakfast, then polish them off with a quart of chocolate milk."

"Sounds like a real charmer." An edge of impatience purposefully crept into his tone.

"Actually, he was more the surly sort when I first met him. I didn't really care for him much in the beginning."

"That so?" Jesse said with the deliberate flatness of the disinterested.

"But I came around. To the point where I fell in love with him."

Jesse looked up at her. When she smiled, his heart broke all over again. He bent his head and busied himself testing the flashlight, searching in the box for extra batteries.

"I think he was in love with me the first time he laid eyes on me." There was a teasing lilt in her tone.

He switched the larger portable light on and off with several sharp clicks. "I'm sure the tales of your teenage romances are fascinating, but we're going to be here awhile, so I hope you have a wider range of conversation than your adolescent crushes."

She turned the box of licorice over and over in her hands. "He liked to play the tough guy, you see. I saw right through it."

"You were remarkably insightful for your age."

"Focused and mature also."

Jesse's lips tilted involuntarily. He stopped before he smiled. But she was right. As a teenager, she'd been no-nonsense, serious, bookish except for a mischievous streak and a smile that turned pretty into beautiful. He'd never understood what she'd seen in him, a boy who'd been brought up to think with his fists first, who'd been taught that any chance of success would have to come from his physical prowess, not his intellectual capabilities.

Until he met Amy. She'd taught him something that no one ever had before. She'd taught him that he wasn't dumb.

"What were you like at seventeen?" She interrupted his thoughts as if reading them.

He leaned down to inspect the portable battery-operated radio he'd taken out of the boxes, fearing the emotions stirred by his memories were revealed on his face. "The same fun fellow I am now."

She laughed, the sound lovely in the dark surroundings. "That's about what I figured."

He felt her study. He lifted out an oil lamp, filled it, trimmed its wick. If the hurricane did hit, they would rely on flashlights, but for now, the lantern's glow would help to soften the room's shadows, lessen fears. He lit the wick, then adjusted it to a controlled flame. He felt its glow coloring his skin, knew its fire was reflected in his eyes. The light spilled out into the darkness. He made his mouth a straight, hard line as he took in the glow coloring her skin, reflecting in her eyes.

A broken tree limb crashed against the window. Amy jumped. When he looked at her in concern, she set her mouth in the same hard line as his. Even at seventeen, she'd hated to reveal any vulnerability. She'd thrived on caring for others, but she'd despised being put in a similar position of needing assistance. He'd seen right through her, too, he remembered. One kiss and he'd stripped her soul bare. And she'd been right. She had had his from the beginning.

"Be good if those windows were boarded up," he said. "Best I can do is duct tape though." He looked up to the second floor. "Have you been upstairs yet?"

She shook her head. "Just in the kitchen. There's some cooking utensils, dishes, not much else. A walk-in storage room, but it's pretty much empty except for a few odds and ends."

Jesse eyed the loft. "The higher ground might be useful if there's a sea surge."

Amy nodded. She remembered news stories of past hurricanes and the rushing water walls formed by the storms' force that could wipe out everything in its path. She had read about fish found three miles inland, moored boats flung against city street lights as if a drunken sailor had gotten confused while waiting for the tide to come in. Like Jesse, she hoped the tornado and maybe some flooding were the worst this part of Texas would experience from Damon. But both of them had been involved in enough emergencies to know only a fool didn't prepare for the worst.

"That is if the winds don't take the loft first," Jesse said. Picking up the small flashlight, he moved toward the stairs and climbed to the second story. Effectively evading any more of her questions, Amy realized.

"You're not getting off that easy," she muttered. She marched toward the steps and climbed to the open upper floor. The room had a sloped ceiling that formed a high peak in the center. It was empty except for some boxes piled in the corner. Amy walked to a row of windows, touching one of the panes to tell where the inside stopped and the outside began, now that the darkening dusk had gone from gray-green to gray-black. She felt the glass tremble with the force of the rain and the wind, heard the roar of the storm, the sounds of unsecured objects crashing against the building. With all the windows shut, the hot air had risen to the loft and it was hard to breathe.

Amy stared past the sheets of rain into the disorienting darkness of the storm with a strange, sinking feeling that the worst was yet to come. She turned to Jesse, stooped beneath the slanted ceiling along one wall.

"These windows should be duct-taped as well," she said.

"We'll want to move most of the supplies up here too."

Amy nodded. If a Category Four hurricane hit on this coast, it was unlikely the building would withstand the winds. If it did, the sea would follow with its own drowning fury.

"The sea surges in California can cause more damage than the initial storm."

"We haven't heard a report in hours. Damon could have easily turned as they predicted, gotten caught up in a tropical depression and become no more than nasty rain and wind." But the eyes he now turned away from Amy said otherwise.

A pile of boxes was stacked in the corner. Jesse bent down, opened the top one and shone the flashlight inside. "Just some old papers." He pulled out a handful, aimed the flashlight at the top one, read it, then the one below it and the one beneath that. "Looks like old bills, business papers." He dropped the bundle back into the box, rifled among the rest of the pile. "Tax returns, business receipts, stuff like that." He opened another box. "Canceled checks in here, some old bills."

When he straightened, Jesse found Amy standing right beside him, a strange expression on her face as if she'd just seen a ghost. A ghost of the past, he feared. He stepped away from her. "Nothing in here to help us."

As he spoke, he replayed the last few minutes to determine if he'd done or said something to spark such intent interest. He had been about to tell her the truth when the tornado hit. Now he was not sure how to begin. If the hurricane was still heading to the coastal plains, it was predicted to make landfall around midnight. He glanced at his watch. It was just after seven. He had five hours. Five hours to tell her the truth.

"It's going to be a long night," he told her.

She nodded as if understanding.

"We should unpack, get settled in." He aimed the flashlight's beam toward the stairs, lighting them for her safe descent.

Amy walked to the stairs and climbed down. The sounds of the storm, the clatter, the muted light and, most of all, the man above her, made her feel she had stepped into a dream. She watched Jesse make his way down the stairs. As he'd looked over the papers in the boxes, she'd seen his lips move while he read. The Jesse Boone she'd known fourteen years ago had had the same habit.

So did thousands of other individuals, she told herself. Was she truly seeing signs to confirm her suspicions, or were these ordinary coincidences fueling her fantasy?

Jesse headed to the boxes of supplies, turning his well-shaped backside to her, and Amy found herself admiring his impressive anatomy.

She mentally shook herself and walked over to join him.

Jesse gathered up the blankets and pillows. "I'm

going to take these into the storage room, see if the shelves slide out. If Damon does hit, it's the safest spot."

"I'll carry some in," Amy said, taking half the bedding from his arms. "I want to get that roll of paper towels in there to clean up a little out here."

In the storage room, Jesse removed the shelves. Amy spread out the blankets, propped the pillows against a wall. She took the paper towels to the sink. The faucet whined as she turned its handle, releasing only a small amount of water before the pipes emptied. When she returned to the main room, she saw Jesse had filled and lit another lantern. The room's glow heightened to almost cozy.

She took the damp towel and brushed off the front counter's layer of dust. As she worked, she hummed a tune, trying to concentrate on remembering the song's words instead of analyzing Jesse's every mannerism.

He glanced at her several times with a furrowed brow. She hummed a little louder, not so much to spike his irritation but to drown out her suspicions, which insisted on gaining strength instead of being subdued. About fifteen minutes went by. Still she hummed. Jesse's glances became more frequent, as if he were waiting for her to begin her inquisition anew and bracing himself for the next round. She hummed merrily in defiance of the storm's fury surrounding them and the questions and confusion within her.

"What is that?" he asked abruptly.

"What is what?" she snapped, startled out of her own thoughts.

"That noise you're making?"

"It's a song." She thought a minute before breaking into a smile. "But I'll be damned if I remember the name." She furrowed her brow in concentration and hummed a little louder, bouncing a bit to the beat as if to shake the memory from her subconscious.

"Is that necessary?"

She glanced at him. He seemed preoccupied.

"No. Outside of food, water and oxygen, little is necessary. But there's a lot we can enjoy."

"Your attempt at a musical interlude, Doc—I'm not enjoying it."

The lines on his face had deepened, and the lanterns' glow shadowed his features. Something was bothering the man.

She smiled, snapping her fingers as she bounced up and down on her toes. "Keep sweet-talking me like that, Sheriff, and I'll sing for you."

He turned back to the boxes as if surrendering. "We'll wait to take these things upstairs. If Damon does hit, the wind will come first, then the water." He lifted the box and set it against a wall.

Lord, she'd thought he would be thankful she wasn't asking any more questions. Not that she was finished. She needed to be certain that the man before her was not the Jesse Boone she knew.

And what if he was?

Her humming stopped.

What if he was?

New thoughts caused chaos in her mind.

What if he was?

She had been so focused on determining if the man before her was the Jesse Boone who had broken her heart fourteen years ago or merely a stranger with the same name that she hadn't thought any farther.

What if it was the same man she'd loved, and yes, she realized with a sobering, almost-terrifying wash of emotion, had never stopped loving?

He looked at her as she stopped humming, the intensity of the flames seeming to sharpen his features, darken his eyes. He watched her. His lips parted as if he had something to say.

What if it *was* him?

"Where's the duct tape?" she asked with a sudden urge to stay busy.

"I'll do that," he said.

She arranged the food supplies, paper and plastic ware neatly on the counter, put a box of disposable cleansing towels from her medical supplies in the bathroom. Jesse finished taping the windows upstairs and down. He returned to the counter, where Amy had pulled over two stools and was wiping the dust off them. He took in her attempts to arrange the supplies. She looked at the large silvery Xs across the windows. Their eyes met.

She smiled as if amused by their efforts. "If Damon does hit, we don't stand a chance in hell, do we?"

He smiled back, knowing she was right. "I'll worry about that when it happens."

Her eyes held steady on his. "What do we do now?"

"Wait."

She barked a dry laugh, exposing the tension inside her. "I don't do 'wait' very well."

"Surprise, surprise," he said as she straightened an already straight row of bottled water. "Unfortunately, the alternatives are slim."

She moved out from behind the counter to a window as if watching would hasten what was to come.

"Are you hungry?"

Surprisingly she wasn't, although it had been several hours since they'd eaten. Nor was she tired, the adrenaline from the day's events overstimulating her system.

"I've got a deck of cards," she heard him suggest behind her. She turned. Jesse had sat down on a stool and was slipping the cards out of their container. He shuffled. "Beats you singing to me."

She sensed he was trying to make her smile. It worked. She walked over to the counter and sat on a stool. "Poker, five card draw. Up to four cards with an ace, three without an ace, jacks wild."

He looked impressed. "And here I figured you for a 'Go Fish' kind of gal."

She tapped the top of the deck. "Deal, cowboy."

"Yes, ma'am," he drawled.

She grabbed the box of pink-and-white licorice from the tidy stack of food, opened it and counted out equal amounts of the candy.

"We're playing for Good & Plenty?" Jesse asked, amused.

"No fun unless the stakes are high."

Jesse's face sobered slightly. "Is that your philosophy in cards or life, Doc?"

"Both," she said, picking up the hand dealt her.

Neither spoke as they reviewed their cards, their expressions serious as they arranged their hands. Amy settled on her stool, gave Jesse a low-lidded look. "What's the ante?"

"Four." Jesse slid the candies into the middle of the countertop between them.

Amy nodded approval as she added her candies to the pile. "Feeling lucky, Sheriff?" She grinned at him.

The smile he gave her almost toppled her off her stool. "Quit stalling. Place your bet and take your punishment."

She laughed easily, the kind of laugh that seeped into a man's bones and turned them soft. One grin and she had him. Jesse would tell her the truth, tell her everything before the night was over, but not yet. He did not know what would happen once he did, but for the moment, he would not worry. He would sit here, the woman he'd always loved across from him, and be grateful. He'd been given a wonderful gift. It might not last long, possibly only a few hours at the most. Plus, he'd already wasted a day trying to keep his secret safe and protect Amy from the truth. A whole day—so much more than he had ever expected to receive. He now realized God in his strange, mysterious ways had answered his untold prayers and given Amy back to him—if only for a few hours.

Feeling lucky? She'd asked him. He looked at her and smiled. She had no idea.

Outside the storm raged around them, the winds thunderous, the darkness almost complete. Inside, in the lanterns' light, Jesse watched Amy study her cards with the intensity she applied to everything. When she looked up, her eyes took a moment to focus. A flash of surprise lit their blue-green depths as if she was startled to see him there. She smiled, turning Jesse to Jell-O, as she laid two cards face down. "I'll take two."

He watched her as she slid over the new cards. Her eyes still on him, she picked them up. Her gaze flickered to the cards, her expression revealing nothing. She inserted them into her hand, shuffled another card to the opposite side. She looked up at him, her hand of cards held close, her smile mysterious. She added two more candies to the pile.

"Feeling lucky," he teased her, wanting the smile to remain on her face.

"You'll rue the day I walked into your tiny town, Sheriff."

He kept smiling as he discarded and drew one card from the deck, afraid if he didn't, the anguish inside him would spill over, out his every emotion. He met her bet.

"Call?" she asked.

He nodded.

"Read 'em and weep, Sheriff." She fanned her cards onto the counter. "Three of a kind. All ladies."

He sighed as he stacked his cards face down. "Beats my two deuces."

"Come to Momma, my little beauties." Amy wrapped her hands around the pile of Good & Plenty candies and slid them toward her. Jesse gathered the cards—including his own hand with a king high flush—into the deck. Watching her delight at winning was worth risking his soul for a white lie.

She pushed four candies into the space between them. "Ante up, lawman." She smiled.

Oh yes, he thought as he added his share to the pot, he'd go to hell and back just for her smile. Their gazes locked, held too long. Their isolation, the intimacy of being cut off from everything except each other seemed to pulse in the air like a living, breathing entity. Her smile turned puzzled, as if she felt the connection but didn't understand why. He looked down, concentrated on dealing a new hand.

"So, are all your family around here, your mom and dad, sisters, brothers?"

Here we go again, Jesse thought. "All that I know about." He wasn't ready to reveal more.

She raised a brow as she looked at him over her hand. "You suspect there's some you don't know about?"

"Just a figure of speech. How many?" He nodded toward her hand, turning the attention back to the game.

She laid her cards down, her eyes staying on him. "Three."

He dealt her the cards.

She slipped the cards into her hand. "How many relatives are around here? And are they all as ornery as you?" She added two candies to the pile between them.

"No one's as ornery as me." He slapped down two cards, picked replacements off the top of the deck.

"How about tight-lipped?"

He slid the cards one at a time into his hand, keeping his eyes on her. "I like to play my cards close to the chest." He met her bet and raised her by two. "Call?"

She shifted her gaze to study her hand. Her eyes raised to study him. "You're bluffing."

She referred to more than the game. "Prove it," he challenged.

He saw the gleam in her eye and realized his mistake. Nothing got her juices flowing more than a challenge. She met his bet and raised it by two. She leaned back with a satisfied smile, enjoying herself.

This time he did only have a pair of threes. She'd done it again. Seen right through him. Fourteen years later and he still hadn't learned a damn thing. He should fold.

He met her bet, raised her three, playing another game now.

He leaned back on the stool with the air of a pleased man. "Take your best shot."

She studied her cards for several seconds before she looked up at him. No smile now. Only an intensity to her eyes that mesmerized him. He did not move, even as she leaned forward and pressed her mouth to his.

Shock rippled through him. Still he did not pull away but leaned into her, tasting her sweet lips and thinking no farther. He heard her own gasping intake of breath and knew she shared his shock. She stood, as if needing to get closer to him, even as they both knew they should pull away, had to pull away.

He rose to meet her, need driving him now as it

drove her. It had always been like that between them. Explosive. Fourteen years and the wide separation that had become their lives disappeared beneath the touch of flesh to flesh, two mouths melded together, opening, tasting, drinking, greedy with a power and drive equal to the storm around them. A storm that moved inside them now.

The cards and candy scattered as he cleared the counter to ease her up onto it, his tongue delving deeper, his hands eagerly touching, taking what they'd ached to do since he'd first seen her. She responded with similar fire, exploring him, her need as agonizing as his. But not like this. Not without her knowing the truth. He had to stop.

Her hands roamed along his shoulders. Anxious fingertips explored his back, his chest, as if discovering a new treasure. He propped her up on the counter. Her legs wrapped around him, pulling him tight to her while their mouths stayed locked, never leaving each other but drinking deeper, the need too great, too long unfulfilled, too long denied.

He had to stop. He would not, could not go on without her knowing the truth. He had to stop now before it was too late. Yet he couldn't.

She reached for his hand and placed it on her breast, pressing her softness into his palm. Her body arched, her legs tightened as if she couldn't get him close enough. He feared it was too late. The crash outside, the tremble of the building that caused her breath to hitch and her body to jerk with surprise called him back, allowed him the second to gain control. He wrenched his mouth from hers, his breathing ragged. Her legs loosened, went limp as a rag doll's as she pulled back from him. He stepped away, needing space now. Her lips were thick from his kisses, her cheeks flushed. He had to tell her now.

"Amy—"

Her eyes lost their glazed look. "It's you. You bastard. It's you."

CHAPTER SEVEN

OUTSIDE, another crash sounded. Inside, Amy's world collapsed. The moment her lips had touched his, she'd known the truth. No man had ever made her lose control the way Jesse Boone had—not fourteen years ago, not now. Even standing before him now, she still wanted him more than she'd ever wanted any man in her life.

"You bastard," she cursed him again. She drew on her anger, fanned it high for fear other emotions would take its place. She glared at him. Inside she could feel herself falling, crumbling like an object that had gotten too close to the fire and was now ashes.

"Why?" She spat the question out at him. Their breathing was shallow, their chests heaving from desire and emotion. "Why?" She began to tremble in her fury. Outside the wind rode high with ear-splitting thunder.

"I was with my father on a job in Salt Lake. He was working off the books, laying pipe in a new apartment complex. I helped out after school, Saturdays, carrying pipe, doing the heavy work. The project was three months behind, and everyone was scrambling to get it done. We were working on the fifth floor. My father sweating joints, me running pipe." He kept his voice level, his gaze steady on her face. His face showed nothing. He'd had fourteen years to tell this story; he could do so without emotion.

"They weren't sure what happened. They think there must have been a hole in the line of the hand-held tank my father was using and gas had been leaking out steadily. Anything could have ignited it, a hot piece of solder, a spark. The tank exploded."

Acid-tongued flames and suffocating smoke. Jesse on his knees, crawling, inching forward. His vision going black as he groped blindly toward his father. Reaching the head, tugging, the flames closing in, the sizzling heat, the smoke.

"The scaffolding hadn't been set properly." His voice was flat, void of expression.

"You fell five stories?"

He released her hand. Her arm dangled at her side.

"Your father?"

Jesse glanced away, then back at her. He shook his head.

"I was in and out of consciousness the first few weeks from the dope to kill the pain. They learned from my father's records that he had a brother, only known relative. The hospital contacted him. He offered to take me in once I was ready to leave the hospital. A few months later I was out of danger enough to be transferred to a Texas hospital."

Amy dropped onto the stool, the assault of emotions draining her.

"When the scaffolding broke, I fell onto heavy equipment. My back was broken in three spots, one leg crushed. The doctors didn't think I would ever walk again. It took six years to prove them wrong."

Amy's medical training told her he shouldn't have walked again. In fact, he shouldn't have survived.

"There were lacerations, contusions, a punctured lung..."

"Your face?" Amy asked softly.

"Shattered by the fall."

She touched his cheekbone. "Reconstructed by plastic surgery."

He nodded.

She drew her hand back from his face and stood, paced a few steps. "All these years. All this time. Didn't you think I had a right..." Her voice quavered. She looked back at him. "Why, Jesse? Why?"

Her expression turned hard. "Even today, did you have any intention of telling me the truth?"

"I saw you this morning and realized you had done as I'd hoped. Become a doctor, created a life for yourself, achieved your dreams. What right did I have to try and turn that life upside down? What would have been the point of telling you the truth and risk hurting you again?"

Amy shook her head. "You don't understand."

"It's been fourteen years. What good would it have done to tell you the truth now?"

"What good would it have done? I would have known the truth. I deserved that much." Her voice cracked. She turned away. "I loved you."

"I loved you, Amy."

She spun around, her gaze sharp. "Don't you dare, Jesse. Don't you dare tell me that you loved me. Do you know how long, how many nights, how many tears…" She broke off, moved toward the windows. She turned her back to him, facing the storm. Her arms wrapped around her waist and she held herself.

"Amy?" She felt the tentative touch of his fingertips on her shoulder. She should step away. She didn't move.

All was black outside. The wind surged stronger than she'd imagined possible.

"Come away from the window, Amy."

At first, she thought it was only her body trembling as she reeled from shock, but the tremors surrounded her now, the floorboards and wall joints shaking from the storm. She stepped away from the window as Jesse asked, and tried to still her body. She could hear thrumming sounds and hard pings when objects hit the sides of the house, as if knocking to come in. She looked at Jesse. His grim expression answered her. If the storm had shifted, it might have missed Corpus Christi, but it had not made it as far as the Mexican border. It was now heading straight for the shore area where Amy and Jesse were stranded. Soon it would be pounding on the front steps. But for now, the hurricane was inside her.

She faced her first love. In the muted light, his scars were still visible. The aftermath of his accident, the pain that would not go away was in his eyes. Now it was her pain too. Added to the fourteen years of questions without answers, tear-filled nights, angry pleas, unanswered prayers. Fourteen years of the pain of a heart missing its other half.

He extinguished one lantern, but left the other until the storm hit, postponing using the portable lights as long as possible to conserve batteries. He faced her again. "The storeroom should be the safest place. There are no windows."

He had not asked her forgiveness. She did not know if she could answer him if he did. The strong and violent emotions had leveled off now, leaving her body physically weak. The wind howled against the walls. The windows rattled. There was not much time left.

She stared at Jesse's face, so unlike the face of his youth. She searched for the boy she knew, saw the man he'd become. All those years lost. A new wrenching pain twisted her gut.

She knew there was a plea in her eyes, and she heard a plaintive keen in her voice as she said, "I don't understand. Why?"

The pain inside her was mirrored in his eyes, eyes she now recognized as belonging to the boy she'd known. She stepped back. The deep blue of his eyes went black with grief. He closed them for a long moment as if overwhelmed. When he opened them again, she saw he had regained control.

"You would have come," he said flatly.

"Yes."

"You would have stayed by my side through every operation, every hateful procedure, every humiliating helplessness."

"Yes," she answered, although she knew he had not asked a question. "I would never have left you."

She meant to hurt him, her anger still too fresh and irreconcilable. The pain in his eyes told her she had done so.

"No, you wouldn't have abandoned me. You would have given up your scholarship, school, your career, your dream of being a doctor."

She said nothing. They both knew it was true.

"For what?" he asked.

"For us." Her answer sparked a fresh flash of pain in his eyes.

"No. I couldn't allow that."

Behind him she saw the windows take on a strange shape, as if bowing inward from the pressure of the wind. Inside her, her anger and pain gathered new fury. "What gave you the right to make that choice for both of us?"

"There was a big chance I would never walk again. Even if I did, it would have been years and years of surgery, hospital rooms, recovery time, therapy, setbacks, frustration, disappointment. I didn't know if I would ever be able to hold a job again. I didn't know if I would be able even to do a simple task like take out the garbage." He paused. "Pleasure a woman, father a child. Is that what you wanted, Amy?"

Her body had tensed as if to ward off the reality of his words. When they stopped, she bowed her head as if unable to withstand any more and answered him.

"I wanted you."

Her voice was small, quiet, contrasting with the

mounting fury outside. The building made a grinding, straining sound against the storm. Amy's heart made the same pathetic protest inside her, unable to accept what she had learned.

Lightning flashed outside the windows. In the brief burst of light, she saw a huge tree upended, its root system higher than the windows, clods of dirt as big as cars shaking from its roots. Amy thought wildly of the people gathered down by the pier and prayed they had come to their senses long before this. And as for the boys…

Jesse grabbed her arm but she jerked it away. "Don't touch me," she hissed. The queer satisfaction she felt at the bleakness that passed across his features was soon replaced by her own anguish.

"We've got to get in the storage room." He blew out the remaining lantern. The darkness inside matched the darkness outside. Disoriented, Amy waited until her eyes adjusted to the full blackness of the hurricane. A light beam cut through the dark. She saw Jesse standing there like a savior. He swung the beam toward the kitchen. The odd pot and pan rattled in the cupboards. Chairs toppled, and cans and boxes fell off the counters as the hurricane pawed to get in.

"The storage room," Jesse yelled. "Now."

She grabbed the small flashlight with her free hand and circled its light around the room and the supplies they'd carried in, as if checking to see what could save her. Nothing. She looked at the items she'd arranged in precise order, now scattered in disarray.

She looked at Jesse. He was watching her, waiting.

From outside came the thunderous gibberish of howls and wails like hell itself.

"Amy?"

She moved toward him, stopping in front of him so close she saw the tension in his muscles, the restrained rise and fall of his chest.

Anger and bitterness were gone from her voice, leaving only defeat. "I wanted you, Jess."

He followed her into the storage room, their lights leading the way. Amy settled down on a blanket, propping a pillow beneath her back. She switched off the flashlight. Jesse's light scanned the narrow walls, high ceiling. He panned it across the kitchen.

"Sit down, Sheriff," Amy said in a flat voice. "Nothing else can be done now."

His gaze fell on her. His expression was hard to read, the muted light making him a mystery. He propped a pillow against the opposite wall. Their legs were drawn up to their chests. Three feet separated them.

"We'll leave the door open for now," he said.

She stared at him. "Tell me more," she said plaintively.

"Amy—" He gentled his voice as if to placate her.

"Tell me everything," she said, steel in her tone. "You woke to vertebral fractures, comminuted fractures of the leg, facial lacerations, intra-oral lacerations, avulsed teeth, fractured facial bones, fractured jaws…"

She laundry-listed the possible injuries as if knowing more, knowing everything could make her understand, could wipe away the loss of fourteen years.

"What was the hospital? Small? Community? Surely, your injuries would have required the skills of a large medical center."

He watched her as she rose on her knees and came closer to him, examining his features with a critical eye. He didn't flinch as she snapped on the flashlight. He remained stolid as she traced his scars, first with the light, then with her fingers, seeing new ones that had been so expertly stitched, they hadn't left a seam. Only the whiteness of new tissue. She turned his head to the left, the right, her flashlight held high, illuminating the scars hidden along the hairline, behind the ears, down the neck.

She set the flashlight down, its light now aimed on Jesse's body. Her gaze locked with his as she unfastened the top button of his shirt. She saw his muscles tense. She undid the next button and the next, pulling the shirt out of the waistband of his pants, spreading it open. A light layer of dark curling hair veed along the muscles, unable to hide the scars. She pushed the shirt off his shoulders, all the way down as she moved behind him. She repositioned the flashlight, then sucked in a breath as she saw the thick puckered scar along his spine. Her professional objectivity failed her, and the woman she was let the tears slide down her face. She reached out, touched the wound. The tension in Jesse's shoulders forced him still.

"Jesus," she whispered. Her voice caught in a sob. She leaned down and pressed her mouth to the wide swath of skin, felt his sharp intake of breath. Her mouth moved blindly up his spinal cord, the tender skin twisted by both injuries and surgery. Her fingers crept up his arms, across his shoulders, as if by touching, tasting his flesh, his pain, she could understand how he could have abandoned her, how fourteen years that should have been theirs had been lost. At last she pulled back and sat on her haunches, shaking with confusion and fear, fury and desire. Then she leaned forward and rested her cheek on his broad back, beautiful in its agony, marked with suffering. He remained still as the wind beat against the walls and she sat trembling behind him. She felt the power that had allowed him to survive his accident.

He half rose and turned to her. She could see the strength in his face now, in his steady expression.

"I'm not saying what I did was right. I'm not saying I didn't know it would cause you pain. But I'm not saying I'm sorry. When I walked into the firehouse this morning and saw you, a beautiful woman, an accomplished doctor, I was not sorry."

She bowed her head. He came to her, crouched down and gathered her in his arms. She could not fight him off even if she'd wanted to. He stroked her hair, his touch light. She'd remembered the passion, the pain. She'd forgotten the sweetness.

"I'm not sorry, Amy."

She laid her head against his chest and wept.

She heard a train coming straight at them. Lifting her head, she looked into Jesse's eyes. The building, its walls shaking and windows rattling before in nervousness, now began to crack. She heard glass breaking, shingles being ripped off, and all around them, the very air shaking with an inhuman force.

"Lie down," Jesse ordered.

She did as he said, lying flat on her stomach, the floorboards beneath her trembling so hard she didn't know how they stayed together. She heard the storage-room door slam. A tree fell, clipped the roof. Amy swallowed the scream in her throat.

"Cover your head." Jesse had to shout above the thunderous fury although he was right next to her. He arched over her, shielding her. Windows blew out, spraying glass across the floors. The storage-room door split, the walls around them cracked. The hurricane had came inside now, pelting the floorboards, their bodies, swirling around them as if to carry them off too, take them away only to discard them, fling them down like garbage, then swoop them back up again until they were beaten and broken and near death.

Amy covered her head with her forearms, trying not to think, waiting it out until it was over, even the slight weight of Jesse's body not stilling her trembling. She thought of her son, the man above her. She prayed for life.

The wind howled with a banshee's glee. The chaos peaked. All around her the world cracked apart, and Amy feared they would not survive.

And then the storm subsided—so suddenly Amy thought it an illusion. She didn't move, not trusting her own senses as she heard the groans soften, the howls hush, the pounding of her own heart again.

Jesse's sheltering warmth moved away as he stood. She pushed herself up from the floor. All around them lay splintered wood, cracked Sheetrock, mounds of pink insulation like cotton candy. Jesse was watching her, looking for injury.

"I'm fine," she said, brushing the dirt off her clothes. He turned to the doorway.

"Wait," she said. His back was covered with tufts of insulation. "You've got stuff all over you." She brushed his shoulders, across his back. He stood still for a second, then shrugged off her hands and drew his shirt back on.

"Doesn't matter," he said.

He was right, she realized as she followed him out of their narrow shelter. They were alive. That's all that mattered.

They walked carefully through the kitchen, picking their way through the debris. Parts of the ceiling had fallen and insulation lay on the floor like snow. Miniature tornadoes had come through the building, knocking over stools, chairs, tables, any object that had gotten in the way. The windows had been blown out, the glass glittering amid the damage like buried treasure.

"I heard the trusses crack but I think they held." Jesse looked up at the second floor. The tar paper beneath the shingles had ripped off, exposing the sky. The stairs had shifted but, remarkably, held.

Amy stepped almost daintily through the destruction, making her way to a wide hole that used to be a window. She looked out. The clouds had parted. Above was a sky so clear, so calm and peaceful it brought tears to her eyes. The moon was a white glow and the brilliant wash of the Milky Way stunned the sky with a light like no other.

Beneath this beauty were the remnants of pure evil. Wind, rains, waves crashing around the edge of the eye. Trees broken, snapped at the trunk or ripped from the ground whole, leaving the landscape bare and ugly. One particularly large tree had gone down, and the Bronco, parked beneath it, had been lifted on its root system and now tilted high above the bombed-out landscape like some crazed symbol of surrender.

Downed power lines crisscrossed the trees. Objects gathered in the storm's fury and cast off at its whim dotted the broken landscape. Parts of boats, the pier, seaweed, a fish as big as a dog were all part of the scenery like a madcap tableau of modern art.

Amy turned to Jesse. He'd picked up a piece of insulation or two, then stopped, dropped them. He looked at her across the ruin. His gaze circled the room and returned to her once more, desolation in his eyes.

Neither had spoken since they'd left the storage room. Amy looked at the man across from her, solid, alive, seeming unreal in this nightmare of destruction. She thanked God for their survival, but her prayers were not over. She was not fooled by the silver sky above, nor the sacred and wondrous silence after so much rage, or the calm and balmy air. The temperature was rising so fast, she felt the sweat bead on the back of her neck. They were smack dab in the middle of the hurricane's eye, and the northern wall was the most destructive side of the storm.

Amy looked at Jesse. Neither spoke. They didn't have to. They knew. The worst was yet to come.

CHAPTER EIGHT

JESSE MADE his way to the window. "Won't be long before the eye passes. The back end of the storm will bring the sea surge." He looked at the ocean, now like glass, the storm at its edges. "Flooding is going to be the problem, along with the winds. We've got to head upstairs to higher ground."

Amy nodded but didn't move.

"Hope we can salvage some of the supplies. The blankets and pillows are still dry. C'mon." He took her arm lightly.

She did not pull away. She let him lead her from the wreckage outside. The fact that the Jesse Boone who'd left her fourteen years ago was here beside her had become secondary to survival now. Her world had narrowed down to this room, this man and making it through the night. She thought of her son. She looked at Jesse.

"I'll get the blankets," he said.

"I'll check out the supplies." She found the boxes beneath dust and wood, slightly crushed but with several salvageable items. She discarded the damaged items and combined the two boxes into one. Jesse met her at the bottom of the stairs. He traded her the bedding for the box. "I'll go up first to make sure the stairs aren't damaged. If they can hold my weight, you'll have no problem."

He climbed the steps, testing each one before putting his full weight on it. He reached the top, turned to her. "They'll hold."

She followed him up. Gaps where the tar paper had ripped off revealed the eerily beautiful sky, but the roof had held. The rain had blown over horizontally. The air was muggy and ripe with the scent of damp plaster and the sea. Jesse went to the gaping windows and looked toward the ocean. Amy joined him. A sudden gentle breeze greeted them. Farther down the beach, it looked clear, but at the eye's edge, clouds hovered.

Jesse rummaged through the remains of the supplies. He pulled out a package of beef jerky and ripped open the plastic wrapping. He handed her a wide slab.

She shook her head. "I'm not hungry."

"Force yourself." He thrust the dried meat at her. "If the surge comes, bringing the tide inland, the water could take everything. There'll be no food, no water until help comes and we can get back to town. Eat."

She took the strip and bit off a chunk of the dehydrated meat. She chewed hard. The dryness of the meat and the dryness of her throat caused the jerky to wad in her mouth. She ground it with her teeth, reached one of the surviving bottles of water and drank. Finally she swallowed the chunk of jerky.

"Eat more," Jesse advised her.

She gave him a long, unsmiling look, but bit off another chunk. He smiled as he peeled another strip from the package. They ate in silence, standing at the window, watching the sea, the moon sliding in and out of the low clouds moving in. They stood as close as they could without touching. The clouds gathered and a sudden gust of cold air caused Amy to tense. She slipped her hand into Jesse's, finding it warm and strong and scarred. The past did not matter at this moment. All that mattered was right now, and the fact that they were alive and unharmed.

At first Jesse did not respond, uncertain, but gradually his fingers wrapped around hers, held them tight. And she was grateful.

The clouds came together more thickly, and the moon was gone. The air temperature fell as quickly as it had risen. The scent of a storm filled the air.

A powerful gust came through the hole where the window had been, threatening to topple them, but they stood strong. Hand-in-hand, they watched with helplessness and awe as the sea rose up high and came toward the land. What they saw froze them. The water was black as ink, the surf rearing up, heading for landfall like a moving cliff. Behind the first wave came another, rising, getting taller, bigger, stronger as it rushed toward the dunes and destruction. Even from a distance, the power was unmistakable and terrifying. The rains broke through again, the black waves and gray sky rising up monstrous, evil, unstoppable. Easily twenty feet, Amy estimated. The eye had passed. The moment of calm was over.

"It won't be long before the waters reach us," Jesse

said. She said nothing, helplessness holding her hostage.

"We're high enough—we'll be safe," he reassured her. "By the time the waters reach here, they'll have leveled off. They'll flood the roads, ruin whatever hasn't yet been ruined, but up here, higher up, we'll be safe."

The rains blew, battering their faces. A piece of debris whistled by. The trusses creaked above them. Amy gave a gasp and watched in horror as the wave slammed into a beach house three-quarters of a mile away, rocking it on its stilts and peeling back the roof like a sardine can. The left side of the house fell away. Only the front stood, unsupported, as if caught by surprise before it collapsed in on itself.

"Amy?" Jesse had not let go of her hand and gave it a gentle tug. "Come away from the window."

She nodded, knowing he was right, and moved with him toward the corner where they had piled supplies. They sat cross-legged on an opened blanket. Jesse unscrewed the top of a peanut butter jar, tore opened a pack of crackers and began smearing them with the spread. He handed her a cracker heavy with peanut butter as if they were on a picnic.

A memory rose up. Another picnic, another time, another life. Two days before her eighteenth birthday Jesse had surprised her by hitchhiking the many miles from Salt Lake City, where his father had gotten a job and moved them both to a few months earlier. He could only stay two days. His father had gotten him work after school on the construction site where he was employed. It was not enough time. It was never enough time. It was all they had.

They'd rented a boat and rowed to a secluded cove carved into Seattle's coast. Their own private island, she remembered thinking. The water had been calm, glittering with the day's sunlight. He'd packed a bottle of sweet, sparkling cider which he'd opened ceremoniously. He'd toasted her. "To you, Amy Sherwood."

Laughing, she'd kissed him, then raised her own glass. "To us." She had never been so happy or certain or young as she'd been on that day. She had not known it then, of course. Life had stretched out before her, and her love was as bright as the sun on the sound. Jesse hadn't needed to ask her wish when she blew out the candles on her favorite chocolate fudge layer cake, which he'd special-ordered from Johnson's Bakery. She hadn't needed to tell him as she'd moved into his arms, the cake and sweet cider forgotten for the sweeter taste of Jesse. Her wish had been in her eyes, the urgent touch of her hands, her body pliant against his with a warmth and fever beyond the day's temperature. She had not known then that even one perfect day such as that was a lot to ask in a lifetime. All she'd known was that she loved Jesse Boone, and to spend the rest of her life with him would not be long enough.

That day was the last time she'd seen him until yesterday morning.

She took the cracker thick with peanut butter. "Do you remember the last time we saw each other? You and your father had moved to Salt Lake a few months back, but you had come for my eighteenth birthday—"

"I remember everything." His features were neutral, hiding any emotion underneath.

"Your accident? How long after that day did it happen?"

"Six days."

"Jesus."

He raised his eyes, looked her full in the face for a count of five, then lowered them once more. He buttered a cracker, topped it with another to form a sandwich and handed it to her. She ignored it.

"When I hadn't heard from you for over a month, I called the number you'd given me. The woman at the desk said you and your father had left weeks ago."

"He was waiting for me when I got back from Washington. Said his buddy had work at a commercial job in New Mexico. Good pay. Work would last months, maybe longer. I was going to call you as soon as we got settled somewhere and I could give you a phone number."

"But then the accident."

He said nothing. What was there to say? One perfect day. Then fourteen years of nothing. She knew it was more than many people had in a lifetime. Amy looked at Jesse. It was not enough.

"That day—"

Amy's words were cut off as lightning flashed, filling the room with an artificial brightness. She saw Jesse in the mocking light, and uncertain, she could not continue. The half hour of calm was over. The storm had rallied. It descended again with renewed violence. As the fury returned, the silvery sky had taken on a green tint, as if ill with the destruction it wrought. The building was shaking, struggling to stay upright, as weary as its occupants.

Jesse fished in the box of supplies and took out a thick coil of nylon rope. He handed several loops at one end to her. "Take off your belt. Thread this through your belt loops."

She did as he instructed, trying to still her hands, which were trembling from fatigue and fear. He removed his belt and snaked the other end of the rope through the loops around his waist. When she finished, he came to her, securing the rope around her waist with a series of intricate knots, then repeated the same on his length. The rope was long, providing several feet for freedom of movement while they waited for whatever the storm had in store for them now. Yet he settled close beside her, and she was glad. She could have easily moved into his arms, but she fought the desire, sitting stiffly upright, her knees pulled up to her chest and her arms wrapped around them. The roof above them creaked, and any tiles not taken before now popped like gunshots. Jesse had fastened the portable light into his belt. Amy had done the same with the smaller flashlight, although the storm's light illuminated more than either of them cared to see.

A loud crack came directly overhead. Amy huddled into herself. Jesse's arms came around her, pulling her tightly to him. If he'd asked permission, she wouldn't have refused. He didn't ask. He brought her to him, letting her take shelter in the strength of his body. The building trembled. She looked into his face. He kept his grim expression averted, although he saw her study. Finally he looked down at her, careful not to reveal any emotion.

He bent close to her ear. "Whatever happens, hang on to me."

Forever, her heart answered. She reached out, her touch tender this time as it found his face, felt the years of pain and healing. She stretched up and placed a light kiss on his mouth. His lips beneath hers responded with a gentle, reverent tentativeness that made her want to weep. It could be a kiss hello or a kiss good-bye. As the wind and sea reared around them, obliterating as much as possible, all bets were off.

A tremendous crack sounded, as if the world were being ripped in two, filling Amy with a desperate fear. The beach house was breaking up all around them. The structure seemed to sway, pitching like a boat at sea.

"She's not going to hold this time," she screamed at Jesse.

"Hang on to me," he yelled. "Hang on to me."

She was thankful he did not say everything would be all right.

Hang on to me.

It was enough to save her.

Huge squares of the roof were peeling back, leaving grave-sized holes. The rain and the wind pelted Amy and Jesse with a brutal carelessness, the gusts seeking to suck them out through the openings. There was nothing to grab on to but each other. The shaking around them became violent. Amy fisted her hands into Jesse's wet shirt and cried his name, although she knew he couldn't hear her. She heard one final crack, and with an almost detached fascination watched the floor beneath them give way like a trap door. For a second, they seemed suspended in air like characters in a cartoon, then, still clinging to each other, they dropped straight down into the black water.

The strength of the surge slammed into Amy. A wave ripped her from Jesse, held her under, rolled her over, then snatched her up, hurtling her into something unyielding. Her legs and arms flailed as she tried to right herself, but the waves kept breaking over her, disorienting her, holding her underwater. She struggled to find her footing, but felt no solid surface. Objects, hard, wet, scratching, bumped into her. She surfaced once, gasping, only to be sucked under again, pulled by the current. Something hit her in the back, knocking what little breath she had left out of her. She searched for the surface, her hands outstretched, clawing at the current. A new blackness, even darker than the storm or the water washing over her, was wrapping around her, pulling her down into its depths. A soft, womblike darkness so easy to slip into. Her arms and legs were like weights. Her movements became less frenzied. Her body went limp, no longer fighting. All boundaries seemed to dissolve. She felt herself melting into the water.

Something jerked her hard, snapping her head back, pulling her with a fresh strength until she broke the surface. She slammed into a wall. She cried out, choking up water as Jesse's arms wrapped around her.

She clung to him, coughing, heaving deep breaths. The wetness that trickled down her face tasted salty—of the sea, but also with the metallic bite of her own blood.

"You're cut," Jesse yelled. He wiped high on her forehead. "It's a gash but not too deep." Holding her tight with one arm around her waist, he tried to dog-paddle with the current, but the waters were too strong.

"I'm fine," she screamed. The irony of what she said hit her. A panicky laugh bubbled up in her chest but was swallowed by a wave that sucked them both under. They surfaced, gasping, the water lifting them, only to suck them under again, rolling them over and over as if hell-bent to wrench them apart. They clung to each other. Fate which seemed calculated to separate them, would not win this time. Survival was dependent on them staying together.

Amy heard an inhuman sound, and was frightened it came from inside her own battered, weary brain. Then she saw a tree float by, a cat high in its branches, screeching its primal rage. Then it was gone, carried away by the water, blending with the ever-changing keys of the wind, shrill as a madwoman's protest one minute, deep as a subterranean monster next, all adding to Amy's sense that the world had become a moaning, heaving house of horrors. She clung to Jesse without shame. Pieces of houses, objects of everyday life—dishes, window screens, a garbage can—coasted by. A section of white picket fence passed by as if the storm gods laughed at the humans' attempts to live happily ever after. She cleaved to Jesse, her very survival dependent on pressing her heart to his. Hadn't it always been that way?

"Don't leave me this time," she yelled, made brave by the fact her words would be swept away by the fearful wind before they reached Jesse. She looked at his face as he held her strong in his arms, even as the waters fought to take them down, jerk them apart. Shamelessly she wished she had made love with him when the house still stood and the world was not a screaming vortex of madness. Damn her pride. Damn his pride. We should have made love, she thought with a wildness rising like the wind. She clutched at him. He responded, his arm tightening, holding her fast against him as if he'd heard her plea.

Don't leave me.

A ceiling beam struck them from behind, but it was traveling in the same direction as they were and didn't hurt them. It moved on swiftly and was sunk by the waves before they could grasp it.

The water took them. Jesse reached out and grabbed a thick branch of a tree that had fallen, stopping their travel. They draped themselves over the limb, leaning against each other, shuddering. The clouds were racing at them at ground level. The sky kept changing from gray to black, black to that odd green. Every few minutes it would ignite with white lightning, spotlighting the trees, cars, various household items as if proud of the destruction it had wrought.

Amy watched in fascination as everything from television sets to shoes came swirling by while the churning surge made its way across the land. Jesse aimed his flashlight beam around them. It bounced off what looked like a pair of red eyes about thirty feet away. Monster eyes, Amy thought, her own eyes widening with terror. He directed the beam back at the eerie gaze. Others were reflected in the light like a hallucination. Then she saw them. Snakes weaved among the low limbs of a tree. Four or five dozen of them, their yellow and black bodies stretched long as if a waking nightmare. Cottonmouth water moccasins. One bite could bring a man to his knees.

Amy looked at the tree they clung too, ready to submit to the surge over snakes. Anything that touched her now made her fearful. She felt something long and cylinder-like brush against her leg and she started, kicking her legs furiously, pulling out of Jesse's hold.

"Snake," she screamed in answer to his puzzled look.

He reached down into the rolling waters and retrieved the length of rope left loose between them. She stilled her legs. She heard the edge of hysteria in her laughter. Jesse's brow knitted into deep lines. He pulled her back to him, his arm tight around her waist, his fist pressed into her rib cage. Through the wet cloth, she could feel the strong lines of his body, the powerful muscles. Lifting her head, she kissed him full on the mouth because he was there. Because she was scared. Because despite the number of times she'd told herself the opposite, she had never stopped loving Jesse Boone.

She kissed him long and deep, pushing her tongue into his mouth with a desire and a desperation, feeling as out of control as the storm around them. She hated the fact she wanted him, that she reveled in the hard thrust of his arousal. She had once believed they'd be together forever. All she knew now was that they were together this moment, her mouth on his, her body pressed to him. Past that, she had no idea what would happen. Life had taught her not to make predictions. She reached up, smoothed her hand over his forehead, trying to ease his worried brow.

She felt the wind drop. At first, she thought she'd imagined it. The kiss ended. She looked into Jesse's eyes, dark with passion and concern. The noise had died down too. She only needed a slightly louder than normal tone to ask, "It's over?"

His brow pleated again as he looked around. The world grew calmer, as if the eye of the storm had returned. It had to be the end. No sooner had her hope flared than the winds struck again, crueler after the false calm. The tree gave a violent shudder as if being twisted under the water. Amy held on to Jesse and together they went down again, plunged back into the rushing water, tumbling, fighting fate. Amy lost her grip, felt Jesse's strong, powerful body slip from her hands. She opened her eyes under the water, saw Jesse's figure, blurred by the water and movement. She reached out toward him, the waters trying to carry her away. She tumbled, turned upside down and lost him. She fought toward the surface, screaming his name as she broke through the waters. A sound hushed her, made her fear escalate. A buzzing that was not animal but man-made. Thirty yards away she saw the loose whip of live electric wires ripped down by the storm. The power grid had not shut down yet.

"Amy."

She swung her head. Jesse was fighting to make his way to her, struggling against the current carrying him in the opposite direction. The rope had tangled around something solid, leaving Amy paddling in place as Jesse tried to reach her.

"I'm caught," she screamed. A wave rose over her, took her down. She dangled like a marionette, thrashed by the water's movement, then was thrown to the surface again. She grabbed on to a branch long enough for the wind to lift her, as if it were fighting with the water for her. The wind lost as the branch snapped and she was sucked back down into the dark flood, her screams for Jesse silenced.

Branches scraped her body. Her head hit something solid. She thought of the snakes, her legs thrashing, kicking out in case the serpents had found her in the hellish night. Whatever had snagged the rope had broken free. She was moving with the speed of the waters and wind, not even the resistance of Jesse's weight dragging on her. With frenzied movements, her hands searched the water, finding the rope that led from her waist, connected her to Jesse like an umbilical cord. She pulled on it hard, bringing it up from beneath the depths. It came easily, the end jaggedly sliced by sharp debris.

She flailed in the water, trying to turn, grab something stationary to stop her runaway motion and allow her to look for Jesse. The cut rope still clutched in her hand, she hit hard against an unmoving surface. She groped blindly, feeling an uphill slope. A roof. She scrambled to gain footing but the pitch was steep and slippery, sending her sliding down into the water again and again until finally she crawled onto its crest. She clung to the roof, her body draped along its slope, heaving gasping breaths of exhaustion.

Jesse.

Buttressed by the roof, she searched around the whirling waters but saw no sign of human life. Electrical lines lay limp across the water's surface. Thank God the power grid's safety had kicked in, turned off the juice. The current would have killed a man instantly.

"Jesse," she screamed. She clung to the roof, wet and shivering, her teeth chattering except when she screamed. She heard a howling as if the earth had answered. Straddling the roof, she twisted her head in the eerie green phosphorescent light to see another cat floating by in a tree's branches.

"Jesse," she cried into the wind and sullen light, her fear becoming fueled by anger now. No sense could be made of finding him after fourteen years, only to lose him again…forever. Her mind could not conceive of a god that cruel. "Jesse," she screamed into the night. A car floated by. She tried to see beyond its windows but doubted Jesse would have crawled inside. It would be too difficult to get out.

"Don't you do it, Jesse Boone. Don't you dare leave

me again," she railed, her fury born of exhaustion and shock and despair. She sat crouched along the roof, clinging to a chimney, refusing to succumb to hopelessness.

She considered her options. She could go back into the water and try to search for him, but if the current had carried him away, it might be impossible to find him. Debris seemed to be coming from every direction, piling against the roof. She saw a baseball cap, small, as if for a boy's head. Amy thought of her son.

She glimpsed something in the odd assortment of objects floating by. She peered more closely, her fatigue and the green light making much indistinguishable or fantastic. She saw a hand, an arm waving as if in celebration.

"Jesse," she screamed, clinging to the chimney so hard her muscles ached and begged for release. Through the roar and the howls and the moans, she heard a faint but sweet sound.

"Amy."

She smiled for the first time in many hours and slumped against the chimney. Jesse, gripping a large slab of siding, was heading toward her. She saw the rope trailing in the water behind him. He crawled up onto the roof, wet, bruised, blood trickling from scratches along his cheek, but very much alive.

Amy clutched his wet shirt. She was shaking so hard she could hear her bones rattle. "I thought…the rope…it was cut…and I thought—" The words were coming out as incoherent and out of control as the night.

"I thought…I thought…" She clung to him now, her

hands feeling his shoulders, arms, chest with a healer's touch but also a touch of wonder. "I thought..."

Her voice was trembling with feeling and she couldn't finish her sentence, overcome by emotions—relief, anger, fear. Her hands clutched his wet shirt again, her fingers fisting the cloth.

"Amy," he said with a tenderness so at odds with the havoc around them.

For the first time in fourteen years, she started sobbing.

"I thought you'd left me again."

CHAPTER NINE

NEITHER OF THEM knew how long they stayed like that, clinging to the chimney and each other. Huddled together, their bodies provided heat as well as comfort. She had cried. He had stroked her hair, kissed her mouth, her cheeks, her forehead until her sobs had subsided. He didn't say he would never leave her again. Now was not the time for promises.

Together they waited for daylight. The wind pressure eased. The temperature rose. The heavy rain was soon only drizzle. The clouds rolled back. Amy and Jesse leaned on each other, their legs pulled up and their chins on their knees, and faced east. The morning broke calm and blue as if proclaiming its innocence of the night before. They had survived the night, the storm. Would they survive the secrets that had been revealed? And the one secret Amy had not yet disclosed?

She straightened her back and gazed out at the crazy waters around them, objects floating by in nonsensical fashion. In the light, the beachfront was like a battlefield. The waters had carried them far up the coast. Several houses looked as if they had exploded or collapsed in on themselves, but two or three on tall stilts remained almost untouched. The only pattern was that there was no pattern. Amy sat, thinking of life's caprices.

As the storm dissolved, the sea had receded, leaving behind only a few feet of water in which to float a menagerie of items, like a Daliesque bubble bath. Piles of cars, boats, houses, furniture and mattresses rose up like ruins.

"The Coast Guard should be the first to come by," Jesse said, surveying the landfill. "Patrolling against looters." He looked at the houses, high on their pilings, that had survived. "We could go to one of those houses. There'd be food. Dry clothes."

He looked at her, his scarred face scratched and cut with the night's terror. She saw the weariness in his eyes and knew the same was reflected in hers. She tucked back a limp strand of hair behind her ear and nodded.

They shimmied down the roof and trudged toward the standing houses. The water wasn't icy or high, but the dampness had reached down to their bones, wrapping them in a chill as if they'd never be warm again. As they approached the houses, they saw the back and side had been blown off the first one, revealing the contents, which were untouched by wind or water. It was like the open back of a child's dollhouse. Even the stairs were intact.

They moved on to the next house. The windows were blown out and shingles torn away, exposing the black tar paper below, but otherwise, it was untouched. Amy and Jesse climbed the stairs and unlocked the door by reaching through a hole where a window panel had been. They entered a wide living room separated from the kitchen by a long, curving counter. Large windows in the spacious room looked out at the devastated houses, the fallen, broken trees, the small hills of refrigerators, appliances, cars and construction materials. Amy didn't realize she had begun to shake again until Jesse laid a hand on her shoulder.

"Let me see if I can find towels, a blanket."

She nodded, although her trembling was not from the cold. It was from fear. Within the house's shelter, she was again struck by how close they'd come to death…and how lucky they'd been to survive. Jesse came back in to the room. His arms were filled with a stack of towels.

"It's amazing they're dry."

"It's amazing we're alive."

He set the towels on the table and shook open a large one. He wrapped it around Amy's shoulders, lightly massaging the length of her arms and back to warm her. "It is amazing," he agreed. His voice was husky. He stepped away from her, selecting a towel for himself. Turning his back to her, he stripped off his shirt and began drying his upper body. She saw the scars again in the new daylight, symbols of his survival. A survival fought for again only hours ago. Fought with her instead of alone. He'd had no choice this time.

He turned, the towel draped around his neck, to find her in front of him. Her hand came up slowly, her fingers tracing the new scrapes and scratches on his face. Death had never been as close as the life that now swept through her veins in a hot rush. She did not know what she wanted or what Jesse wanted. She did not know what would happen in the days to follow. All she knew was that she wanted to feel this alive for the moment. Alive. Her senses heightened. Her fatigue recharged with pure adrenaline. Jesse Boone was right here in front of her, beneath her touch. Anything seemed possible.

"Amy—"

It was a question. She touched a forefinger to his lips. "Don't say it." Words that would stop her.

"Amy…"

She moved closer, leaned into him. "Don't say it." she whispered.

"Amy…" The question was weakened by desire and a need too long aching inside him. Amy knew because it was the same for her.

Her body fit against him. Only a breath of hesitation now. He still had not touched her, as if he'd given up the right long ago. She felt the hard tension of his body, the way his breath held tight in his chest, the desire. She lifted her face to his.

"Amy," he said, just as she'd imagined for fourteen years. A single tear slipped down her face.

"Jesse…" she whispered in a trembling breath.

He bowed his head and captured the word in his mouth as he touched his lips to hers. Her mouth quivered beneath his. He lifted his mouth and whispered her name again. His gaze asked a final time.

"I don't know what we can have, Jesse," she answered, her voice shaking with desire and need. "All I know is we can have this. We can have now."

He bent his head to her. He did not ask again. They did not speak again. There was no need. Everything was said with a look, a touch, a shuddering breath, a sigh. The innocent light of the new day bathed their skin, the warm air caressed them. They stripped off their wet clothes, left with nothing but their aching, throbbing need. He stepped back, his hands running up and down her arms, and she felt bereft at even this temporary separation.

She stood before him and let him look at her now. No longer a teen with a newly formed figure but a woman of thirty-two who had won battles also. Her scars were not so many and hardly visible. A softening of the belly stretched by childbirth, a fullness to the breasts. The waist was not so narrow, the skin not as tight and unblemished as in youth, but otherwise she was slim and strong. With a wildness, an eagerness of the young and the innocent inside her. The way Jesse had made her feel fourteen years ago. The way she'd never thought she'd feel again.

Raising her hand, she laid it on his abdomen, felt it contract beneath her palm with a sharp intake of breath. With a growl, he pulled her to him. Cupping her face, he claimed her mouth, plundering it with long, slow, voluptuous strokes of his tongue, claiming her the way no other man ever could. She drew him into her mouth, nipping at him, wanting to own him as he already owned her.

It wasn't enough. It couldn't possibly be enough. But it was more than she'd dreamt possible.

They moved as one across the room and fell onto a

long, deep-cushioned sofa. She heard her own voice, a moaning, triumphant, powerful sound like the wind that had ravaged them throughout the night. A guttural groan answered her. The wildness was inside them. Jesse ravished her mouth, drawing the breath from her body and making it his while her hungry, eager hands explored every inch of heated flesh.

Her skin was like fire everywhere he touched. He moved his mouth down her throat, opened it on a breast and drew her inside with a fierce need while his hands cupped her buttocks and lifted her against him. Still it wasn't enough. The hunger between them was too great. Fourteen years of pain and desire and dreams stripped away the gentleness, exposing a raw, aching, overwhelming need. She wrapped her legs around his hips. He lowered the length of his body, and with a soul-wrenching groan, entered her soft and willing body.

Amy cried out her own sound of conquest. They'd beaten fate, not once, but twice. She opened wide in triumph, taking him in deeper and deeper while the dark ripples of sensation spread through her. Her body hugged him in possession and with unbridled pleasure. Her muscles contracted, pulsing as he drove into her. They moved together with wordless pleas. She wanted to remember everything. The taste of salt on skin, the wondrous relief of his muscled body, but the sensations blended, became warm and wet, hard and soft. Need. Urgency. They met in a crescendo, a shattering climax that drove through her like a lightning bolt and exploded. She cried out. Their gazes locked. Her heart split wide open.

It was like seeing the clouds roll away and the blue sky of morning rise triumphant after the night's attack. It was like coming home. Even as exhaustion and satisfaction swept over them, his lips moved over hers, against her scratched cheek, her damp hair, as if the chance might not come again and he had to get his fill now. They lay in each other's arms like two lovers, as if fourteen years had never separated them.

But it had.

Even now, as they lay sated and together, a sorrow ran through Amy. A sorrow for what they had missed, for what Jesse had missed, the sacrifice he had made that he didn't even realize yet. She would not deny her love for him. It had always been a part of her. Even when she didn't know what had happened to him, when she feared him dead, when she'd hated him, she had loved him. She had never had a choice. Her heart had been his from the beginning. It could not belong to anyone else. But there were other considerations now besides Jesse and her.

She looked at him, naked to her soul. "I dreamed of this."

"You were supposed to forget me, get on with your life." Gruffness filled his voice.

"You never thought, maybe late at night, or in the early dawn, there was a chance? We could be together again?"

"I did." He paused. She traced the curve of his shoulder.

"It's all I thought about the first seven years after the accident. Getting well enough, strong enough to go to you. Not as a cripple but as a man."

"And?" she asked when he didn't continue.

"I found out your address in California. I called the phone listing."

She stared at him.

"Your husband answered."

She looked down at the finger where her wedding band had once been. "If he hadn't…"

"It was too late."

She idly ran her fingertips up and down his arm. The question hung in the air between them unspoken, neither anxious to know the answer. *Was it still too late?*

Later they could be brave, but not now. Not when they'd only just found each other again.

They spent the next several hours in each other's arms, alternately making love and holding each other, trying to erase the years apart. Even though it was late afternoon, they heard the boat engines too soon. Too much had been left unsaid.

"The Guard must have made it to the beach." Neither of them moved. Their gazes locked but neither spoke. Finally Jesse rose to a sitting position. "We should find some dry clothes, get dressed."

She sat up. "Yes, we've got to get back." She stood, started toward another closet to look for clothes when he grabbed her hand and pulled her back against the length of his body. Cupping her face between his palms, he looked at her as if he feared it was the last time he would see her. He lowered his head, captured her lips one last time.

"Thank you," he whispered against her parted lips as if it were already over.

Was it? she wondered. She had no answer.

She found an oversize sweatshirt, a pair of bike shorts and rubber thongs. For Jesse a T-shirt, sweatpants and sneakers a little too small. He scribbled a note with his name and telephone number to the homeowners, detailing the clothes they had borrowed and asking them to contact him so he could reimburse them. They stepped out onto the deck and waited until the motorboat faced their way, then flagged their arms.

The boat pulled along the shore as Amy and Jesse made their way down the deck steps to the beach.

"I'm Sheriff Jesse Boone from Turning Point," Jesse called to the two guardsmen as they came near. "This is Dr. Amy Sherwood from Courage Bay, California. Came in with a team yesterday morning to assist during the hurricane."

"You two were out here on the beach last night?" one of the guardsmen asked as they climbed into the boat.

Jesse explained that they'd been looking for a group of teenagers when they were stranded.

The men shook their heads. "You two are damn lucky."

Amy looked at Jesse. "We know," she said with a rare smile.

"We can bring you in through the laguna, hook you up with a vehicle, but you'll probably have to go north and backtrack if you want to get home. Even then, roads might be impassable."

"It's worth a try," Jesse told them.

The boat sped north toward Corpus Christi which

except for heavy winds and rains had escaped the worst of the storm's wrath. But along the way, even from a distance, the scenery was a wasteland of shattered homes, destroyed dreams. Houses were no more than flat stacks of debris. Wires hung like snakes from telephone poles. Crushed cars were piled on top of each other or protruded out of the water. Above, the sun shone fierce and high, the sky a brilliant, bold blue; below, devastation.

"Do you know how far in the storm hit?" Jesse asked the men.

"It made landfall farther south than expected and moved inland forty, fifty miles or so, but it hit hardest along the shore. You folks saw it at its meanest. We'll be cleaning up this one for some time."

Jesse nodded, his face grim as the boat sped by the miles of houses tipped on their sides, ripped from their foundations. "Any word on the area around Turning Point?"

"Storm did a good amount of damage, but reports are it weakened as it headed inland. You're seeing the worst of it right now."

Jesse expelled a breath. His disconcerted expression was the only sign of his fear for his town and its people. He was a man who revealed little emotion, a fact that underscored the depth of his feeling, Amy thought. She knew. Over the years, she too had trained herself to keep her emotions under control. Until last night. She glanced at Jesse, her heart as vulnerable as fourteen years ago. It was not a comfortable feeling. She wrapped her arms around herself, hugging the oversize sweatshirt to her body, and forced herself to focus mentally. There would be people who needed her help. She could not afford to be distracted by emotion.

The men brought them in by a bridge where groups of people had already gathered, walking, wading across the rubble, only to be met by military jeeps forming a barricade to the beach. They looked as weary and confused as Amy felt, their faces bleak, stunned, disbelieving.

"They want to see if their homes still stand," one of the boatmen said. "And protect them if they do against the rains they're forecasting for tonight."

"They'll have a long wait," the other said. "Too dangerous to have residents traipsing through the flood waters. There's already been enough damage."

"No deaths, though," the other noted.

"Not yet," his companion said with a fatal air. "It'll stay that way if people don't lose their heads."

Like the men, Amy knew that often more deaths occurred after the actual storm than during it, due to human error. The dangers from the storm were far from over.

The boat pulled up to the shore. "Sheriff and doctor from Turning Point," the man told his colleague as he approached the boat. "Found them out on Padre Point."

The man looked at the couple. "And you lived to tell about it? Good for you. Bastard of a storm, excuse me, miss."

"I have to agree with you," Amy reassured the man.

Another man in military fatigues came up and joined the circle. "Sheriff Boone. Sorry to see you under such circumstances, but glad you're in one piece."

Jesse shook the man's hand. "Good to see you, Hamp. Must be bad to bring you from the base."

"It's a mess but it could be worse," the man said. "My men and I came to lend a hand." He cast a quizzical glance at Amy.

"Amy Sherwood." She extended her hand.

"Captain Hamilton Voss, ma'am." He lightly took her hand. Amy grasped his in a firm grip. "But you can call me Hamp."

"Amy is a doctor with the Courage Bay emergency team that came into Turning Point yesterday to help out."

Hamp gave Jesse a speculative gaze. "How'd you end up on Padre Point?"

"We got caught in the storm when we went looking for my cousin's boy and his friends. There hasn't been news of any others found out on the beach?"

"No reports I've heard of." He looked at the other men. They shook their heads. "But communication is still down."

"Hope that boy used some of the sense the good Lord gave him and headed back when he saw it was getting rough," Jesse said.

Hamp cracked a wry grin. "He's probably hoping the same thing about you."

"We were on our way back when my vehicle got flattened by a tree. Fortunately we weren't in it at the time."

"You've shown Miss Amy here quite a time. This will be one trip you'll not likely forget, right, ma'am?"

"It has been memorable, Captain." She exchanged a look with Jesse.

"Problem is, now we need to get back to Turning Point," Jesse told the men. "Our emergency services were stretched thin before the storm. That's why we brought in back-up from Courage Bay. I'd like to get back to my people as soon as I can."

Amy heard the term *my people,* which told her that Turning Point was home to Jesse. From what she'd seen of the residents, he fit in well—stubborn as sin and full of pig-headed pride. He'd made a life here, as she had in Courage Bay.

Hamp scrubbed a hand across his face. Amy suspected that, like the rest of them, he'd had little or no sleep.

"Travel is tough. Most roads are blocked. They've started clearing some of the major routes, but it's slow going. Could take a good four to five hours to go ten, twenty miles. I can get you a set of sturdy wheels, but I'm not certain how far you'll get. Even if the trees and debris have been cleared, flooding could be a problem."

Jesse hesitated. A glance her way told Amy it was out of concern for her.

"We'll take our chances, Captain," she said. "If the roads need clearing, we'll have to clear them."

Hamp gave her the amused look of a man who thought females were a separate race and should be relegated to sitting prettily or serving pleasingly, not running around disaster sites with lawmen. "The little lady has made known her wishes, Sheriff. What do you say?"

"If you can spare a vehicle, the doctor," Jesse put extra emphasis on Amy's title, "and I will be on our way."

Hamp frowned. "Let me see what's available."

"He's not a bad guy," Jesse said as the other man moved out of earshot. "Just old-fashioned."

"I've dealt with men like the captain and lived to tell the tale."

"I have no doubt." A grin pulled at the corners of Jesse's mouth.

Amy had been independent for so long a time, she'd forgotten how a man could make her go soft and needy. She and her ex-husband had functioned more as a team. They'd coordinated their schedules and shared companionship, but she hadn't been made to feel "need." Twenty-four hours with Jesse and all that hard-fought independence had dissolved in a matter of minutes. She didn't know what the future would bring for the two of them, but she did know Jesse had moved into her heart again, lock, stock and barrel. Except this time, she was not so naive as to believe love was all that mattered. And what about Ian? How could she bring Jesse into his life without knowing where their own relationship was going?

Hamp returned. "I've got an all-wheel drive with a V-8 that should plow through anything. Still can't promise how far you'll get."

"I don't ask for promises, Hamp. Thanks for your help." Jesse shook the man's hand, clapped his upper arm.

"Thank you, Captain." Amy offered her hand.

"You two be careful. There's as much danger now as during the storm."

"You and your men take care of yourselves also," Amy said. "Doesn't seem to be any short supply of heroes in these parts, but I'd still hate to lose one."

The captain cracked a grin. "Heroes come in all shapes and sizes, Doc. Some even come in pretty packages."

"Are you flirting with me, Captain?" Amy smiled back, knowing she'd won over the man.

"Since when was telling the truth a sin? C'mon, you two, let's get you on your way."

The trio walked to the SUV. The captain opened the door for Amy. Smiling at him, she pulled herself up into the seat, then let him close the door behind her.

"Thanks again, Hamp." Jesse patted the steering wheel. "I'll see she gets back to you as pretty as she left."

"Just see you get this one back to Turning Point as pretty as she left." The captain winked at Amy.

Jesse pulled out slowly, heeding the people milling around the bridge.

"He's a charmer, huh?" Amy referred to the captain. "I believe he fancies himself one."

She gave Jesse a grin before returning her attention to the road, which was narrowed by branches and tree trunks lining its sides. The road was one lane until they reached the highway, where four lanes had been reduced to two. Fortunately there was little traffic.

They fell silent, taking in the landscape. Uprooted trees, snapped tree trunks, buckled concrete, ripped power lines. The wind had shorn so many trees, signs and buildings that the vista looked barren and alien. They were rerouted several times due to closed roads. The detours forced them to head northeast instead of west to Turning Point.

"We'll have to go up to the areas not hit by the storm, circle back and come down from above." Jesse fiddled with the radio's buttons. The reception was becoming clearer as they neared the untouched areas of the northern coast. Reports of the disaster monopolized the broadcasts. In some of the hardest-hit areas, power was already predicted to be out for a week or more. Clean-up would be much longer. Relief efforts were already underway, and residents were urged to stay where they were. The reports continued; the stories repeated. Occasionally a new item was added.

It was past sundown when they reached the areas barely touched by the storm's heavy rains and winds. Jesse reversed their direction to head southwest toward Turning Point. He spoke little, anxiety evident in his expression. Amy studied his profile, thinking of the revelations of last night. And the secret that still lay between them. She had to tell him, but now was not the time.

As they headed back into the area hit by the hurricane, the roads became flooded in spots, high enough to stall an ordinary vehicle, but the all-wheel drive sailed through the waters, parting them cleanly down the middle and leaving a foaming trail in its wake. Debris blocking the roads slowed their progress. Sometimes they were able to pull over and clear the heavy branches, but if not, they were forced to backtrack to an alternate route. At last they neared the county line.

Amy recognized a road sign, except now it was bent flat to the ground. She saw level land where a barn with a high silo had stood the day before. They passed a gas station, its storefront blasted clean off. She glanced at Jesse. He concentrated on the road, his lips pressed in a straight white line. She turned back to the view outside her window. The Turning Point she'd arrived in yesterday was no more.

CHAPTER TEN

CAPTAIN VOSS had been right. Turning Point hadn't been hit as hard as the coast, but it was all a matter of degree. *Destruction* had become a relative term in southwestern Texas. The floodwaters hadn't arrived here with the slamming force of the surge, but the nearby river and its creeks had flooded. The waters were receding now, leaving behind mud, silt, drywall crumbled by dampness, insulation only good for mold-breeding spores.

The road Jesse and Amy traveled was awash in a foot of water, which the vehicle easily sliced through. Amy figured they were heading to the firehouse, but then Jesse took a turn in the opposite direction. The houses were spread farther and farther apart, the surrounding fields large ponds, and any crops were ruined. The waters rose higher until Amy feared they could go no farther, but then they leveled out over the fields, forming a wet wasteland. A farmhouse, a barn, several outbuildings sprung up along the horizon. Jesse swung into the farm's long drive.

"This is my Uncle Frank's place. Clare moved in here with the boys a few months ago. She tried to hang on to her house after her husband left, but things got too tight on her cashier's salary. She started waitressing on the weekends, but then Michael started giving her trouble and she didn't like the idea of leaving the boys unsupervised on the weekends. She moved back in with Uncle Frank and Aunt Edna about two months ago. She's still got her hands full with that older one, though."

"I gather that from what little I know of the boy," Amy remarked.

They pulled up in front of the large farmhouse, untouched by the storm except for several shallow puddles the size of small ponds across the front yard. The light from several lanterns or oil lamps glowed in the windows. Amy and Jesse got out of the vehicle.

"Two weeks ago, he threatened to run off to his father's in California. Clare said she had to bite her tongue not to tell him that if his father wanted him for more than one month of fun and games over summer vacation, he would have made it known."

Amy shook her head. "Teenagers. They're a trial and a half."

"I know I was no angel." He fell silent, the reference to the past dropping an uncomfortable tension between them that broke Amy's heart.

"Luckily I straightened you out."

Jesse lifted his hand as if to touch her, but then returned it to his side. He stepped toward her, narrowing the space between them.

"Did I ever thank you for that?" His breath warmed her damp flesh.

"I doubt it. You were an ungrateful cuss then, with a chip on your shoulder big as Seattle."

"Then I met you…"

Amy looked at him. *Then you left me.* The unspoken words remained between them, as tangible as the summer heat.

"Thank you, Amy."

"You're welcome." She felt ridiculous, unsettled by the hammering in her chest and the need shooting through her veins as if they had not lain together only hours ago, meeting each other's needs until both were too sated to move, to do more than breathe in the other and feel blessed.

"If you're as tough on your seven-year-old as you were on me, he won't stand a chance—"

"Uncle Jesse."

A child's call interrupted the moment. Jesse turned, smiled and waved at the youngster splashing through the puddles to be scooped up into his strong arms and held high above his head.

Amy watched Jesse lift the boy, the child's expression adoring.

"He's not seven, Jess," she said softly, although she knew Jesse was out of earshot. "Our son is thirteen."

A young woman stepped out onto the porch. The sallow color of her complexion and the severe style of her hair, pulled back off her face, left her just short of pretty. She folded her arms across her waist, cocking one hip as she watched Jesse and the boy. A smile crept across her face, and Amy saw that she had been very pretty at one time. The woman looked past Jesse to

Amy, the smile still on her face. She stepped down off the porch. As she passed Jesse, she rubbed his arm. She reached Amy and extended her hand.

"I'm Clare, Jesse's cousin, and you must be the doctor from California. Thank you for coming to Turning Point. I'd heard you went looking for my son?"

Amy nodded. "Jesse was worried sick the boy and his friends would get caught in the storm."

"Michael's here, safe inside, thank the Lord. Not that he didn't get a good tongue-lashing when he got home. But I've been wearing out the floorboards worried about you and Jesse. You both are a sight for sore eyes. My boys and I, well—" Clare looked away, then back at Amy. "We've had quite a year. If anything had happened to their Uncle Jesse or to you, I wouldn't have been able to forgive myself."

Amy did not want to add any more weight to the burden this woman already carried on her slight shoulders. "We're fine. Just fine."

Clare surveyed Amy, seeing the scratches, bruises and ill-fitting clothes. "Bet it was a hell of a night." She smiled faintly.

"It had its moments," Amy said softly as Jesse joined them. The child resting his head on his uncle's shoulder examined Amy curiously. Clare rubbed Jesse's arm again. Amy could see these people loved Jesse. She was grateful that after his accident they had been there to care about him.

Jesse put his arm around Clare's narrow shoulders. "C'mon, Clare, don't be getting all mushy on us, right, Shane?"

"Mushy, yuck." The child agreed with a firm nod.

Clare gave the males a tired smile. She leaned against Jesse, accepting the support he offered.

"So, your brother's here?" Jesse asked.

The little one nodded. Clare's smile vanished.

"A group of them, Michael, Lenny Driscoll, Pete Abbott, Nick LaPierre, drove down to the coast to catch some waves." The boy's mother shook her head in a gesture familiar to all parents of teenagers. "They caught them, all right."

"We found a part of a surfboard along the side of the road."

"They had trouble securing the boards as the winds got stronger. Michael lost control of the board coming in on a wave. Got a nice gash on his leg from the rudder and slammed good on the head. Fortunately one of the other boys was nearby and pulled him to shore. Thank God, the tow didn't take him. He used the beach towels and his own shirt to stem the bleeding."

"He was knocked unconscious?"

Clare nodded. "Maybe it slammed some common sense into him."

"He's alert now?" Amy asked.

"Oh, he's alert all right. And complaining because there's no electricity. Child goes into withdrawal without video games or a computer. Only thing he's happy about is there'll be no football practices for a while."

"No signs of abnormal sleepiness?"

Clare looked at Amy. "He's a teenager. The boy could sleep around the clock if allowed."

"What about blurred vision, nausea, vomiting?"

Clare shook her head.

"Sounds like he just got a nasty bump on the head, but I'd like to check him for a concussion or head injury."

New worry etched the other woman's face. "Yes, of course. Let's go in."

As they turned to the house, Amy saw a tall man with the look of a life of hard physical work and simple pleasures in his calm gaze. He came down the porch with an easy gait, a man comfortable in his body and his surroundings. He met the group halfway to the house and put his hand on Jesse's shoulder.

"Son, I'm happy to see you whole and in good health." The man nodded at Amy. "You too, ma'am. When we learned you went looking for Michael and hadn't been heard from since, it was a long night waiting."

"Uncle Frank, this is Dr. Amy—"

"I know who she is." The man's face wrinkled with welcome as he smiled at Amy. "Nice to meet you, ma'am. Edna says for you all to come inside. No electricity, of course, but I got the kerosene grill going, heating up a kettle right now."

"That's where we're heading, Pop," Clare said. "The doctor wants to take a look at Michael."

The older man turned to Amy.

"I'm sure he's fine," Amy reassured him, "but any time there's a blow to the head, you want to watch for concussion or a head injury."

The group moved inside. "Of course," Frank agreed. "Category Four storm and the damn fool goes surfing into the middle of it."

"He's sixteen, Uncle Frank," Jesse said. "That's all."

"That's enough." The old man sighed. "Not that I'm so old I don't remember pulling a few crazy stunts myself."

"We've all got our stories to tell, Pop," Clare said as they stepped inside. The farmhouse had a well-lived-in air. Even in the dim light, Amy could see that the fabrics on the furniture were faded, but the pillows were plump and piled high. Family photos decorated one wall and a large quilt covered another.

"The storm skipped you then?" Jesse said.

"We were some lucky," his uncle said. "A few tiles on the roof popped and the winds were like the hounds of Hell, but the house is still standing."

"We'll be saying extra prayers tonight," an older woman said as she came into the room. Her plump, sturdy figure and kind face with its deep laugh lines revealed she shared her husband's ease with life. She wrapped her arms around Jesse and the child he still held. She moved on to Amy without hesitation, enveloping her in a strong embrace.

She stepped back, her hands still clasped on Amy's shoulders. "A couple of those prayers will be for you," she told her with a smile. "I'm Edna Boone, Jesse's aunt."

"Amy Sherwood."

"Well, c'mon in the kitchen," Edna said, slipping her arm around Amy's shoulders, "and we'll see if we can find something to feed you. We're limited without electricity so we'll have to be more clever than usual."

"Where's Michael?" Clare asked.

"In the kitchen also." Edna led Amy toward the hall. "I set him to peeling some potatoes. K.P. duty. He's mumbling about it, but busy hands do a boy good."

Edna led Amy into an open, airy room with high ceilings and a chrome table. Chrome chairs with vinyl seats circled the table. The kitchen set had been copied and called retro in California, but this one was original, enjoyed for its function rather than funky charm. "Your husband must be worried sick about you, Amy."

"I'm not married." Amy gave the woman the answer she was fishing for. She recognized the boy at the table from the photos in the other room. Even though he was sitting, she could see he was lanky like his grandfather, but not fully grown. His body fit him like a too-big suit, forcing him to hunch his shoulders over the pile of peelings in a stainless-steel bowl that matched the table legs. A mean red welt primed to blacken had already risen on his forehead.

The boy glanced up, his expression the sullen, disinterested mask universal to teens and criminals about to be interrogated. He took in Amy without curiosity.

"Michael, this is Dr, Sherwood," his grandmother introduced. "She came all the way from California to help out during the hurricane. She and your Uncle Jesse went to Padre Point searching for you last night before the storm made landfall."

"Two more people who were worried about you," Clare chastised.

The boy gave his mother an impatient look. Clare crossed her arms across her chest as if donning protective armor in preparation to do battle. "Not only did you put yourself in danger with your foolish antics, you put them in danger as well."

The boy glanced at Amy and Jesse. "Sorry," he mumbled, lowering his gaze to the potatoes.

"I'd like to take a look at your forehead, Michael," Amy said. "Check to make sure that bump is just a bump."

Setting down a potato and the peeler, the boy watched her as she rounded the table to where he sat. She pulled out a chair, met him eye level.

"Face me, please," she instructed. "Any blurred vision?" She felt the boy's forehead, along his neck and glands for swelling.

The boy shook his head.

"Nausea, vomiting?"

Again the boy shook his head.

"Headache?"

"A surfboard cracked my skull. It wasn't pretty."

Amy smiled. "Was the pain sharp, shooting?"

"Nah. Just like I got dropped on my head."

"Has the pain increased or subsided since you got beaned by the board?"

"It's dull now."

"Take any medication?"

"Nah."

"Good. In case of a head injury, even a simple aspirin could have consequences. Abnormal sleepiness?"

The boy looked at her. "My mom thinks so."

Again Amy smiled. "Outside of normal teenage sleep patterns, which do tend to be excessive."

The boy shook his head. "You're from California?"

"Courage Bay," Amy answered. She moved the small oil lamp on the table closer. "Follow my finger with your eyes, please. Look up. Look down. Stand, please."

Amy rose with the boy to find he was several inches taller than she was.

"Is that on the coast?"

Amy nodded. "Right on the ocean. Not far from Los Angeles."

"You surf?"

"No, sir. Not enough hours in my day, but I have some friends who do. Put your arms out at your sides, please. What was the biggest wave you caught yesterday?"

The boy smiled, the wave gaining size in his memory. "Had to be fifteen feet easy. But it was an even bigger one that took me out."

"How'd your friends fare?"

"They got bounced around, probably sore as sh—"

He caught himself. He glanced over at Clare, who glared at him. From the corner of her eye, Amy saw Jesse swallow a smile.

"But you got the worst of it."

"Lost my board, but my dad will buy me a new one." He chanced another look at his mother, who remained silent, arms crossed.

"Raise your arms to your sides," Amy instructed. "Close your eyes. Touch your right finger to your nose. Now your left. Great. You can open your eyes. Your mom said you got a good cut on your leg?"

"When I lost control of the board, the water was

rough. I tucked my head, pulled in my legs like my dad taught me—"

Amy heard Clare sigh.

"But the water was like mad-crazy and the rudder gashed my calf. I wrapped a towel around to stop the bleeding."

"Did that work?"

"Yup."

"I'd like to take a look at it."

The boy pulled up the leg of the flannel lounge pants popular among both sexes his age. The cut was open but the blood had coagulated, leaving a fresh, bright red strip. "Good. The bleeding has stopped. Stitches won't be necessary." She turned to the others. "There doesn't seem to be any damage."

"Except it was a foolhardy stunt to pull in the first place," his mother pointed out once more.

The teenager grinned sheepishly. "C'mon, Mom, I'll bet Grandma and Grandpa could tell me some stories about things you did when you were my age."

"I didn't surf during a hurricane warning and get knocked on my backside." Clare rubbed her forehead and turned even paler as the events of last night hit home. "You could have drowned."

"Well, I didn't," the boy mumbled in true adolescent fashion.

"Maybe next time you'll use some of that sense the good Lord gave you," Clare said, infusing her words with anger. "In the meantime, apologize to your Uncle Jesse and the doctor here. They were stuck on the coast last night, trapped by the storm, looking for you. Do you realize what could have happened? Christmas, we were lucky."

"I'm sorry," the boy mumbled, the defiance dissolving a degree as he looked at his uncle and Amy.

"Now, finish up those potatoes," Clare ordered. "After that, I'm sure your grandparents have some other chores for you to do."

His disdainful expression returning, the boy picked up the peeler and the potato he'd been working on. Scowling at the vegetable, he began to peel it.

"Jesse, let me make you and the doctor something to eat. Like I said, we're limited without electricity, but I can whip you up something."

Jesse shook his head. "I appreciate it, Aunt Edna, but I can't stay. It's late now and I've got to get into town, see what has to be done."

Amy nodded in agreement.

"Frank himself was talking about heading into town to lend a hand, but surely not much can be done until daylight without electricity."

"They'll have the generators running," Jesse said. "Plus, I want to be on hand for any calls that come in."

"Well, you've both got to eat or you'll be no good to no one." Jesse's aunt moved to the cupboards. "I'll start the coffee, put it into a thermos. I'll wrap up some sandwiches for you to take with you. Clare, while I do that, you take Amy upstairs and see if you can find some clothes that might suit her. She looks about your size."

"Thank you, but I have some clothes I can change into at the fire hall. I wouldn't mind freshening up a bit, though. If you have a spare toothbrush, I'd kill to brush my teeth."

Clare smiled at Amy. "Sure. C'mon."

Clare picked up a lantern and a flashlight, and the two women left the room.

"Nice-looking woman," Jesse's uncle observed. He looked at Jesse.

"Smart, too. A doctor," Jesse's aunt added. "And single."

"She's a little old for Michael, don't you think?" Jesse said. The boy glanced up. Jesse winked at him in silent partnership. "You got an extra peeler or a paring knife, Aunt Edna?" He pulled out a chair opposite the boy and picked up a potato. Michael smiled.

"Of course she's too old for Michael." Edna handed a peeler to Jesse. "But not for you." She patted Jesse's shoulder maternally. "Time you settled down."

Jesse picked up a potato. "I'm settled, Aunt Edna."

"Settled with a woman. Start a family."

Jesse peeled the thin skin off a potato. He didn't argue.

CLARE HAD LED Amy to the bathroom in the upstairs hall. Placing the lantern on the counter, she set out towels, toothbrush and toothpaste. She opened the mirrored medicine cabinet and told Amy to help herself to anything else she might need. She was sitting on the bed, waiting for her, when Amy returned.

"I feel like a new woman."

Clare smiled. "Looks like you got thrown around some by the storm."

Amy looked down at the bruises and scratches on her body, the cut on her knee. "Nothing serious."

Clare stood. "He's a good man." She sent a sidelong look at Amy. "Jesse."

Amy didn't answer. She didn't need to be sold on Jesse.

"My boys adore him."

"So I gather. He was lucky to have family to take him in after the accident."

Crossing her arms, Clare leaned against the doorframe. "So he told you about that?"

"It was a long night. We had lots of time to talk."

"He doesn't talk about it much. The other men that were there told my dad about it, how Jesse ran into the explosion to save his father. His dad was already dead, of course."

Amy frowned. "I thought Jesse was with his dad when the explosion occurred?"

Clare shook her head. "He was on his way down for supplies when the tank blew. He ran right into the blaze. No one could stop him. He dragged his father's body out. Was trying to bring him down when the scaffolding went." Clare shook her head. "My dad never had much use for his brother. Heck, I didn't even know I had a cousin until Jesse came after the accident. But Jesse loved his father. That's part of the reason he's so good with my boys. He hates the thought of them growing up without a dad."

Amy and Clare returned to the kitchen a few minutes later. Amy had brushed her hair and braided it at the back of her head. She'd washed her face, her cheeks pink from the scrubbing. Even in the dim light, Jesse saw where the night had taken its toll. More than one purplish bruise marred her thighs. Long scratches cut across her arms. He hated the fact she'd been battered by the storm, but he sensed she wore those bruises and scrapes as triumphantly as he wore his own. She was talking to his aunt, when she suddenly turned and looked directly at him. For not the first time in the past two days, Jesse felt his heart stop, then start again.

They stayed long enough for Edna to pack them sandwiches, a thermos of coffee and a container full of homemade chocolate chip cookies. She packed a second basket of food for Frank and Michael, who decided they'd also head into town to see if they could help others who hadn't been as fortunate as them. The women hugged Amy good-bye, and even Michael said thank-you without being prompted. The women and Shane stood on the porch to watch them off. Frank and Michael were putting supplies in a pickup truck as the SUV pulled away.

"It might be safer for them to stay put until more clean-up has occurred," Amy ventured.

"I agree," Jesse said, downshifting, "but try and tell Uncle Frank that. Better off not to argue. He'd go anyway."

They fell silent as Jesse steered the vehicle around deep puddles. They had gone only a mile when he turned left, then left again and crested a hill. The view would be spectacular in the daytime, Amy thought. That image was marred as the car's headlights illuminated a pile of rubble from what once must have been a house. Walls had been ripped and shredded, exposing what was left of the contents. A refrigerator lay flat, thrown at least a hundred feet from the house. Heavy beams crisscrossed Sheetrock and piles of wet pink insulation. A lone tree trunk stood left of the rubble, its leaves and branches torn away. The tree had probably shaded the house.

Leaving the headlights on, Jesse parked and got out without a word, his gaze fixed on the wreckage. Amy followed him. She knew this had been his home even before she saw the mailbox ripped from its post and thrown carelessly amid the rubble, a number and road name stenciled on its side. Beneath the address, Boone.

Hopelessness fell on her hard, threatening to take her down. She might have been mired in the storm's waters again, struggling not to be sucked under. She braced her shoulders and called up a righteous anger, blinking away the tears that welled in her eyes.

Jesse squatted down, his broad shoulders stooped as he sifted among the wreckage. He pulled out a brass doorknocker, staring at it as if it were a rare jewel. Amy stepped toward him over the bits and pieces of his life scattered among the ruins.

She crouched beside him. "Jesse, I'm so sorry. This was your house, wasn't it?"

She placed a hand on his upper arm. He tensed beneath her touch, then straightened, moving away from her. He wouldn't look at her. "It's only a house. Wood. Glass."

"It was your home."

Still he did not look at her. "It was a house." He

moved farther away from her, kicking at the rubble. She stared at his back and thought of what she'd learned from Clare only moments ago. How Jesse had tried to save his father, almost securing his own death in the process. Afterward, he'd sacrificed his own desire so that she could achieve her dream of being a doctor. Playing the hero came naturally to him. What was hard for him was accepting help from others.

She stared at his back. *Let me in, Jess.* She moved toward him, stepping gingerly among the timbers. He stepped away. He did not want her help. Not today. Not fourteen years ago. Thoughts of a possible future together seemed as vulnerable as the building that lay around them.

"We'd better head into town." He gave a final soft kick to a beam. "I'm sure there's plenty ways they'll need our help." He waited for her to start toward the vehicle.

She looked around. She had so many questions. Had he lived here long? Did he build this house or buy it? What color had he painted the kitchen walls? Had he brought lady friends here? Cooked them dinner? Led them to his bed? Fourteen years. A lifetime. She said nothing, just looked at him. *Let me in, Jess.*

"Ready?" He started toward the vehicle without waiting for her. Perhaps, as he'd believed fourteen years ago, he was protecting her. And he had. But then, as now, he was also protecting himself.

She was almost at the edge of the wreckage when she saw a flash of bright green. She bent down and brushed away the damp splinters of wood until she pulled out a small stuffed frog in a faded tuxedo. She smiled as she shook it out, dusting off dirt and tufts of insulation. She'd given it to Jess their first Valentine's Day together attached to a big red heart balloon lettered My Prince. She remembered he'd blushed. Mr. Tough Guy.

He was waiting for her at the driver's door. His gaze took in the stuffed frog in her hands. Fourteen years fell away.

CHAPTER ELEVEN

IT WAS AROUND MIDNIGHT when they reached the center of town. They were silent as they passed blown-out storefronts, a pickup truck tipped on its side, yards littered with an absurd array of objects. Amy saw a rocking chair, an ironing board. A few roofs had been carried off; others had lost only their tiles, leaving them with a bald look. Silhouetted in the darkness, a man and a teenaged boy, both in hip boots, were sloshing their way through puddles. Their flashlight beams were pointed toward a barbershop at the end of the street. An uprooted elm had missed the roof but sheared off the metal awning. It lay thirty feet away, flung against the front of the post office. Amy remembered the gaily-striped barbershop pole that had caught her attention as they'd come into town yesterday. It was nowhere to be seen.

Jesse released a long breath. His features revealed defeat before they altered into an expression of somber determination. He slowed the vehicle as they reached the man and boy, then parked, and got out. Amy did the same. Jesse turned at the sound of her door opening. "There's no need."

"Maybe not." But she hadn't come here to sit and watch from the sidelines. He should have learned that by now. She rounded the vehicle, meeting Jesse at the other side. He flicked a glance at her and shrugged his shoulders as if to say "Suit yourself," but she saw the grudging respect in his gaze.

The boy and man came toward them, the same firm set to their shoulders as Jesse wore.

"Tom. Alex." Jesse laid a large hand for the briefest moment on the teenager's knobby shoulder.

"Sheriff." The man nodded toward Jesse. "Ma'am." For a moment, no one spoke, as if there were no words adequate.

The man put his hands on his hips and looked around. "It could be worse. Heard it practically leveled territories along the coast."

Jesse nodded. "It did."

Jesse's answer brought a long look from the man. "You were there?"

"We went down looking for Clare's boy Michael and his friends. Michael's brother, Shane, had called to let me know the boys had taken off for the coast with their surfboards strapped to the car's roof."

The older man glanced at his son. "You know anything about that?"

"A few of the boys were talking at football practice the day before, saying if the storm came, they should ditch practice and ride some big ones." The boy shrugged. "But practice was cancelled anyway yesterday. That's all I heard."

"And you two got stuck on the coast?" The man

shook his head. "I'm glad you made it back to us in one piece, Sheriff. And you too, ma'am."

Amy extended her hand. "Amy Sherwood."

"Dr. Sherwood came in with the others from Courage Bay to give a hand during recovery," Jesse explained.

"God bless ya, Doc." The man pumped her hand. "We do pretty good on our own two feet but are always glad to have another pair of willing hands. I'm Tom Roscoe and this is my eldest, Alex. Wasn't much Chief Kannon and the volunteers could do last night when the storm reached us, but Turning Point will sure be grateful now for every extra pair of hands we can get."

"How's your house, Tom? Storm do any damage?"

"Knocked an elm on the shed and tried to shake the house off its foundation, but thank God, she stood firm. Helen didn't wait to see if the storm would turn or peter out into a tropical. As soon as she heard Category Four, she grabbed the girls and they headed to her sister's house in Charlotte. Alex and I stayed behind to haul things to the upper floors, nail plywood over the windows." He looked at his shop. "All in all, we were pretty lucky, I'd say. How'd your property make out?"

Jesse shook his head. "Not so well, I'm afraid. Not much left but a lot of waste to be hauled away."

"Sheriff, I'm sorry to hear that you were hit hard." Tom's eyes darkened with concern.

"Houses can be rebuilt."

"That's right. We'll gather up all of Turning Point and have an old-fashioned barn-raising. We'll have a roof over your head in a weekend."

Jesse smiled. "In the meantime, how about I give you a hand cleaning up?"

"Thanks, Sheriff, but I've got the boy here. We can manage just fine. I'm sure Chief Kannon needs you more than we do."

"That's where we're heading," Jesse said. "Dr. Sherwood will be at the first-aid station set up at the firehouse if you come across anyone requiring medical attention. I'm going to check in at the firehouse, then head back out."

"Doesn't look like Gladys made out too good," the barber observed, pointing out the twisted metal frames once filled with plate-glass windows. Diva Dominion—the sign Amy had enjoyed yesterday as they'd passed by in the van—was gone. Domed metal hair dryers lay across the street among two-by-fours and shattered glass, their helmets upside down and full of water.

"Better get going," Jesse said, unsmiling.

When they reached the fire station, they found it unharmed except for the water covering the parking lot. The other town buildings had also escaped damage.

Amy and Jesse parked and waded through the deep puddles. The buzz of generators greeted them, and they saw that the bays for the emergency vehicles were empty.

"They're either responding to calls or out patrolling, looking for downed power lines, sewage and water main breaks. No one should have been on the road, but still, motorists could have gotten caught in the flash flooding," Jesse noted.

In the front hall of the station house, several men slept on cots. Ruth, the dispatcher, set down a coffee cup and rose to meet Amy and Jesse.

"Damn, now there's a sight for sore eyes. After you two headed to the coast, all hell broke loose. Good to see you, Sheriff. Doc." Smiling broadly, Ruth looked from Jesse to Amy. "How you two doing?"

"We survived," Jesse answered. "How's things here?"

"Emergency workers have already been mobilized, heading out to the harder hit areas. Our squads are out now assessing the situation. Not much we could do last night when Damon hit but head for shelter, sit on our behinds and curse the damn storm. And that's exactly what we did, although I had to practically threaten to go out and hogtie that stubborn chief of ours before I could get him to head to the shelter."

"If there's anyone he'd listen to, it'd be you, Ruthie," Jesse said.

Amy saw a faint blush steal across the stern lines of the woman's face.

"Storm wasn't even supposed to strike here, but guess it got a good look at us and decided to say howdy. We only got the tailwind but that was enough."

"What about serious injuries?" Amy asked. "Any casualties?"

"Had to chopper Bill Thompson out to the hospital in Alice to check his heart, but the only casualties reported so far have been material," the dispatcher answered. "Had a scare with a member of your team." She looked at Amy. "The trauma nurse."

"Cheryl?" Amy felt the blood drain from her face.

"She was coming back from a call and got lost trying to take a shortcut. She was on that old bridge not far from where the Hansen barn burned down ten years ago."

Jesse nodded in recognition.

"She was on the radio to the chief, trying to get directions. He told her to get off the bridge. He heard something cracking, the woman screaming. Then we lost the connection. Chief was afraid the current had taken her. He and a team searched for hours."

"Oh, my God." Amy covered her mouth with her hand in horror. "But she's all right?"

Ruth nodded. "Noah Arkin got through on the radio just a little while ago. He was heading to his clinic with a truck full of animals when he saw the car being swept down the river. He jumped in and pulled her out just before the vehicle went under. Says she was unconscious, but her pulse and breathing were steady. The road back to town was already washed out so he took her to his clinic until the storm passed."

"I thought Turning Point's only doctor was in Houston recovering from a heart attack?" Amy asked, confused.

"He is. Noah's a veterinarian," Jesse explained. "You say the woman's okay?"

"Noah said she was disoriented when she finally came to. Hit her head pretty hard in the fall and at first couldn't remember anything. Not even her name."

"Amnesia?" Amy asked.

"Only temporary. By the time Noah was able to radio in, he said her memory was starting to return.

Other than a few bruises, he says she's okay, but the roads are still flooded out, making travel impossible. Hope they'll be clear by morning."

"What about the other members of the team?" Amy asked.

"The paramedic that went up with Jolene to Rock-a-Bye Ranch—"

"Nate?"

"Don't remember the fella's name—"

"Nate Kellison," Amy said.

"They had a little trouble when they got to Lily's. The baby was breech, but between the two of them, the delivery turned out successful. Little girl. Weighed more than nine pounds."

Jesse whistled low.

"And Lily fretting about bringing their prize bull in before the storm hits."

"The one Gabe just brought home?"

Ruth nodded. "The animal was out on the open range. They lose him and there goes the breeding program. Jolene told Lily she'd bring the bull home. The paramedic thought both of them were crazy, but he was determined to go out with Jolene to search for the animal. Then the storm hit. We haven't heard anything since, but ten chances to one, they saw the storm coming in and holed up at Jolene's ranch next door. Don't worry, Doc, if your friend is with the chief's daughter, he's in good hands."

"And vice versa," Amy added.

"Good enough."

"Still, the chief must be worried sick about his daughter."

"I'm sure he is, but he's not one to let on."

"What about Micky Flynn?" Jesse asked.

"He and the female firefighter—"

"Dana?" Amy interjected.

Ruth nodded. "They brought that bunch of Boy Scouts in. Micky made Dana go back to his place for a break. You just missed them. Most of the rest of the volunteers are out also. It's slow going. The outer areas to the south were hit hardest by the flooding."

"I'm heading out myself now," Jesse said. "Uncle Frank and Clare's boy Michael were on their way in when I left their place."

"How'd they make out from the storm?"

"It missed them."

"There's good news. How 'bout your place?"

"Well...I was always talking about remodeling. Now I'll have the chance." Jesse downplayed the loss of his house, uncomfortable with other people's concern.

A burst of static sounded from the office off the main room. "We got the auxiliary radio going but it goes in and out, uncooperative as my first husband."

As if on cue, the radio crackled again. A disembodied male voice filled the room. "One of the volunteers slipped with a chain saw. Avulsion to the lower left extremity. Tissue torn away from the body. Possible nerve damage."

"Let them know I'm back," Amy instructed the dispatcher. "Have him ambulanced here to the first-aid station."

Ruth complied, relaying the instructions to the rescue worker on the other end of the call. When he signed off, Ruth turned to Amy and Jesse. "They're on their way."

Amy started toward the door.

"I'll be right back," Jesse told the dispatcher. He followed Amy. Once outside he called her name. She stopped and turned to him.

"I'm going to head out myself shortly," he said. He moved toward her. "If you need anything, have the dispatcher radio me."

She nodded.

"I'll see you when I get back in. I'll probably be bunking down in my office temporarily. You'll be here?"

She nodded again. He stood as if he had something more to say. She waited for him to continue. He gazed at her but said nothing.

"Amy..." He could not continue.

She smiled and laid her palm on his cheek, dark with a day's growth of beard. "I know, Jess. We need time to talk. Time we don't have right now. I hope we'll have a whole lifetime to figure this out."

He leaned down and kissed her lips.

"In the meantime," she whispered to him, "I'll be here, waiting."

They heard the siren's wail. He kissed her once more, deeper, harder, then let her go.

An appetizing smell surprised Amy as she opened the door where Cheryl had set up the first-aid station. A large pot of soup simmered on a camp stove. Amy familiarized herself with the triage area, finding bandaging and splinting equipment, examination instruments, tubing, catheters, oxygen, saline. She had finished scrubbing up and was pulling on sterile gloves when the rescue squad members wheeled in the patient, giving Amy his vitals as they brought him in.

"Direct pressure didn't stem the bleeding," one of the attendants said. "We had to use a tourniquet."

Amy checked the pressure and placement of the cuff, then cleansed the skin around the wound with a hydrogen peroxide solution and irrigated the deep gash with saline. She looked for any shards of glass or wood embedded in the cut and tested for nerve, artery and muscle function. The man's color was pale but his blood pressure and pulse were stable.

From the supplies, Amy extracted a syringe. "I'm going to give you something for the pain," she said, deftly filling the needle and administering the medication. "Then I'll numb the wound itself and close it with stitches. There is some damage to the connective tissue envelope around the muscle so I'll stitch that up as well." She looked the man directly in the eyes. "Afterward, you'll need to keep the area clean and dry to prevent infection. The stitches will come out within a week to ten days, but it takes six weeks or more for the cut to heal fully. And you'll need a tetanus shot."

She saw the man's facial muscles relax as the painkiller took effect. "Any questions?" She smiled her reassurance.

"Just fix me up, Doc, and I'll be grateful."

"All right." Amy reached for the local anesthetic. "Let's do it."

Shortly after she'd finished stitching the man's

wound, other patients began to arrive. Many came grudgingly, prodded by a spouse's nagging. Most were certain they didn't need a doctor's care and were only wasting time when they could be useful elsewhere. Amy pointed out more than once that they would be useful to no one if they neglected their health. Fortunately, most of the injuries were easily treatable. Any life-threatening injuries had already been choppered out to the Houston trauma center. Amy was kept busy treating the garden variety of general traumas common-place after a disaster. She saw cuts, abrasions and muscle tears, a few mild cases of hypothermia, neck and back complaints from minor accidents when drivers lost control of their vehicles. In between cases, she'd check with the dispatcher or try to catch a quick nap, only to lie on the cot wide awake, listening to the constant buzz of generators and chain saws in the distance. Sitting up after another failed attempt at sleep, she saw the night paling. Shortly before, Mitch had stopped in to see how everything was going and if she needed anything.

"More soup and sandwiches," she'd told him with a smile. "The ladies' cooking works as many miracles around here as anything modern medicine can provide."

The chief patted his generous waistline. "There's something I know all about."

"And a silo-sized coffeepot wouldn't hurt either."

Mitch Kannon's smile eased the weariness etched in his face. "I thought only Texans insisted on everything being bigger?"

Amy adjusted an IV line. "Hey, until yesterday, I only drank herbal tea and honey."

"So we're converting you to Turning Point's down-home ways already?"

Amy smiled thoughtfully. Although she'd grown up in a small town outside Seattle, she'd always been so anxious to move away and create a life outside the area's narrow boundaries that the town had never seemed like home. After Jesse left, it had become a place filled with too many memories. Courage Bay, with its sea and fair weather and brave, caring people, was a wonderful community, but Amy knew she'd ended up there primarily because of Aunt Betts. If it hadn't been for her aunt's generosity and help, Amy would have never been able to attend medical school and raise her child. She thought of Jesse. Their child.

"Lord knows, Turning Point and the other towns around here could use some smart, bright, young medical professionals such as yourself and the others who came in with you." The chief interrupted Amy's thoughts. "Rumor is Doc Holland has been talking about retirement. Guess the heart attack got the man to thinking he might not have as much time left as he'd like. If that's the case, he wants to spend it with his wife and family and on the golf course. Can't say I blame him, but the loss is going to leave Turning Point in sore need of medical services."

From what she'd witnessed, Amy sensed that Turning Point's residents, even with their stubbornness and "can-do" attitude, would readily agree with the chief.

"This is a nice little town," the chief continued. "Good people. Solid values."

Amy smiled. "Are you recruiting me, Chief Kannon?"

He smiled back. "Just giving you something to think about, Doc."

"I'm flattered, but—"

"Just think about it, Doc. That's all I'm asking."

She thought of the past forty-eight hours. Jesse. Ian. "I'll add it to the list."

Mitch nodded. "Fair enough. I'll get word to the school to send out some more soup and sandwiches. The ladies will probably be grateful for something to keep them busy. Last I heard it was fairly quiet up there, thank the Lord. I'm heading out now to meet the chopper coming in to pick up Hal's wife, Beth, and fly her to Houston. Hal's one of our volunteer firefighters."

"What happened?" Amy asked.

"Apparently she cut an artery on a broken window but managed to make it to Noah's. She'd lost a lot of blood and Noah had to operate for fear she'd lose her arm. Lucky for everybody your friend Cheryl was there. I'm hoping the road has been cleared enough to get out there myself. Cheryl says she's just fine, but after her swim in the river, I want to see for myself."

"Don't let her snow you. Medical professionals are the last to admit something might be wrong with them."

Mitch winked. "If she gives me any trouble, I'll bring her to you."

"I'll be here," Amy assured him. "And, Chief?"

Mitch stopped and turned back to her.

"I know you haven't heard from your daughter, but Nate is one of the best," Amy said.

The chief nodded. "As is my daughter."

"I'm sure they're both safe."

"That's my prayer."

After Mitch left, Amy debated lying down once more, deciding it would be useless. Once the sun came up, she could never sleep. Fortunately her internship had trained her to get along with little or no sleep for long periods. A man came in and she wrapped suspected broken ribs, recommending the patient get the area X-rayed as soon as the roads were passable again. The sun was high now, the heat heavy and rich even in the early morning as if in apology to the sky's fury only hours ago. The rescue squad's radio sounded. Expecting Dana, Amy was shocked to hear the voice of Courage Bay Hospital's Emergency Attending, Rachel Browne, patched through from the control center communications system.

"Amy, we've been trying to reach you since yesterday. We finally got through—"

Amy went cold all over in a fine sweat. "Ian?" she asked as the bottom dropped out of her world.

"No, Ian's fine. It's your Aunt Elizabeth. She was brought in yesterday complaining of unbearable pain from a headache. We discovered an aneurysm. They were in the process of opening the skull when the aneurysm ruptured."

Despising the weakness that made her limp, Amy bent her head. She clasped her hands to stop their trembling. Tears splashed onto them. She could not ask.

"They clamped her off, but she lost a lot of blood. Then the healthy veins and arteries began to spasm. They elevated the blood pressure to force the arteries to stay open, but it didn't work. She suffered a stroke."

Amy covered her face with her hands, tried to remain steady. "She's alive."

"She's in a coma, Amy," the other woman said.

Amy took a deep breath, trying to check her emotions. She needed to think clearly.

"Where's Ian?"

"He was at a friend's skateboarding when it happened. One of your aunt's friends had come by to pick her up for Tai Chi class and found her nearly blind with pain and brought her to the emergency room. I had my husband, Guy, swing by and bring Ian to stay at our house, so don't you worry about him."

"I'll get a flight as soon as possible and be there. Rachel?"

"What is it, honey?" Rachel was admired for her calm, competent manner, but it was her compassion that made her a truly remarkable doctor and person. The concern in her soft voice almost broke Amy.

"Tell Aunt Betts I'm on my way."

CHAPTER TWELVE

THE PILOT of the chopper had been radioed to return as soon as he dropped off Cheryl's patient. He got Amy to the airport in minutes. From there, she'd taken a direct flight to California. With the time change, it was not even noon yet as she turned onto Washington Avenue toward Courage Bay Hospital.

Jesse had still been out patrolling and assisting with cleanup, so she hadn't been able to contact him before she left. The chief promised he would explain her abrupt departure. She didn't like leaving this way with so much unfinished between them, but she had to get to Aunt Betts. Phone lines could be down for who knew how long, postponing any immediate chance of talking to him. Even when communication was restored, the matter she needed most to discuss with him was not something she wished to reveal over the phone.

It would have to wait, she told herself as she parked in the employees' lot and took the elevator to ICU. She nodded to colleagues but didn't pause as she headed to the nurses' station. One of the senior nurses filled her in as they walked together to Aunt Betts' room. The surgeon had removed the part of Bett's brain that had died during the stroke and put in a shunt to reduce the pressure. Medications were being administered to suppress seizures that would jar her head and increase the swelling.

Amy reviewed her aunt's chart, asking questions about her condition and care. She did not falter until she stepped inside the hospital room. Her aunt lay on the bed, her eyes closed, her expression peaceful as a ventilator mechanically breathed for her. Fluids were being pumped through IVs into her body to support blood pressure and heart rate. The nurse discreetly disappeared.

Amy moved to the bed, checking lines, monitors. She placed her fingertips along the underside of her aunt's wrist, felt the beat through the thin flesh. Her leg muscles went lax. She knelt by the bedside. Her hand stayed on the pulse, which was remarkably strong. Its life source was artificial, yet as she touched the small throb, Amy could not stop herself from hoping. She covered her aunt's still fingers with her other hand.

"I'm sorry, Auntie Betts," she whispered, as if afraid to wake her. "I'm sorry."

She looked at the unmoving body. Another person she loved struck down physically. And she hadn't been there. She bowed her head and wept silently.

Her tears were spent but her head still lowered when she felt a gentle hand on her shoulder. She looked up and saw Rachel. Amy straightened and stood, brushing away any traces of her tears, embarrassed to have been seen so vulnerable.

"I heard you got in," Rachel said softly.

Amy nodded. "I was lucky to get a flight out fairly quickly." She glanced at her aunt, then back at Rachel, but she could not speak. She looked at her aunt again. "We see it every day, but…"

Rachel put her hand on Amy's shoulder again. "I know, honey."

Amy looked at the other doctor. "There's little chance, is there?" It was a question not even worthy of a first-year med student.

"When the swelling goes down, the pressure releases…" The woman hesitated.

"I'm sorry. It was foolish to ask."

"Amy, every doctor has seen miracles. I have. You will, too."

Amy nodded, turning her gaze back to the woman lying unmoving on the bed. *But not this time,* she thought.

"Is there anyone I can call for you?" Rachel offered.

"My mother," Amy answered. "She should be here. But I can call her, thanks. And Ian, of course. I need to collect him from you."

"Don't worry about him. He's no trouble whatsoever. On the contrary, he's a natural with the baby. You'd think he was the big brother."

Amy managed a small smile. "He never did have the chance to play that role. He's probably getting a kick out of it. I'm anxious to see him."

"He's worried, of course. About you and his great-aunt. But Guy and the baby are keeping him occupied He's wonderful with the baby, Amy."

Amy heard Rachel's pleasure. Rachel and Guy's baby was adopted. The child's mother, Guy's former stepdaughter, had died giving birth. When the baby immediately had begun experiencing cardiovascular abnormalities, Guy had suspected an inherited disorder. Knowing his former stepdaughter had no such health problems, he and Rachel had searched for the baby's father and were able to confirm Heath had inherited a little-known genetic disorder called Noonan's Syndrome.

Rachel glanced at her watch. "My shift is over in a half hour. Why don't you grab a bite, make some calls, then I can drive you over to see him. Or if you prefer not to leave the hospital, I can have Guy bring him over."

"I prefer he come here. If I left, wasn't here and something…" She was stammering.

"It's no problem, Amy." Rachel touched her arm. "Let me go call Guy now. You're welcome to use my office phone for any calls you have to make."

"Thank you, but I have my cell. I'll ride down in the elevator with you."

They separated when they got off the elevator and Amy headed outside. Cell phone signals could interfere with monitors and other medical equipment.

She reached her mother and told her the news about Aunt Elizabeth. Her mother assured her she'd be there as soon as she could get a flight. Amy told her to leave a message on her cell phone's voice mail with her arrival time and she'd pick her up at the airport. After Amy hung up, she sat on the bench outside the hospital for a few minutes. She closed her eyes, tilted her face toward the sun, summoning strength. Wearily, she rose and headed back inside.

EVEN AFTER the accident, Jesse did not remember his body being in this much pain. Of course, time had dulled the memory, and there'd been the relief of massive dosages of pain medication.

He'd worked all day, helping to clear roads, detour traffic, patrol outer-lying regions for stranded or injured residents. Phone lines in many areas remained down. Radio communication was sporadic but improved. The high school was beginning to empty out. Although evacuees were advised to stay put for another few days until the roads became more passable, the late shift in the storm had left many evacuated areas undamaged and residents were anxious to get back to their homes. Those who had lived where the storm had hit were equally anxious to see what damage had been done to their properties. Only fleetingly Jesse thought of his own house, reduced to rubble. It was the first real home he'd ever had. He'd designed the building himself, adapting basic floor plans. He'd known every carpenter, plumber, electrician and laborer employed in the construction, often working side by side with the crew. He'd deferred to Aunt Edna, Clare, and his female friends when it had come to the interior decor. The house had been modest but well-built and efficient. Yet despite his involvement and satisfaction with the house, it had always remained just that. A house. It was missing the magical ingredient that made it a home.

And at night, when he sat rocking on the front porch, his mind would drift to memories of Amy and he would remember that once he'd been in love and it had been perfect. And a loneliness would settle on him like the summer's high heat. He'd known too many such nights in that house. He would not cry now at its demise.

He pulled up in front of the firehouse. Despite the late hour, lights powered by auxiliary generators were on in many of the town's buildings. Sleep for the residents of Turning Point had become a secondary commodity.

As he got out and closed the driver's door, Jesse spied the stuffed frog in his worn but jaunty tuxedo that Amy had propped on the console between the two seats. He smiled for the first time in many hours. He headed for the fire station. He longed for a shower and a meal, but, most of all, he longed to see Amy's face.

When he stepped into the building, he smelled the soup kept warm on a camp stove, saw the cots and medical supplies efficiently arranged in the first-aid area. Fortunately, he had not heard of too many serious injuries throughout the day. Most complaints were minor enough to be attended to out in the field. He hoped Amy's day had not been too stressful and she'd been wise enough to use the down time to get some rest.

Jesse saw Mitch talking to a volunteer from the rescue squad. He scanned the room. He did not see Amy. He moved toward the two men.

Mitch turned as Jesse approached, shot him a tired smile. "About time you came in for a rest." His face sobered. "I saw your house, Sheriff. I'm sorry. One of the hardest hit in the town."

Jesse picked through the sandwiches in plastic wrap piled on a platter near the soup. He chose one thick with ham and cheese, unwrapped it and took a generous bite. "I'll rebuild."

"Sure you will," Mitch agreed. "In the meantime, where are you hanging your hat? There's an extra room at my place, and I'd be happy to have you."

"Appreciate the offer, but for now, I'll probably bunk down right here so I'm available if any emergencies come in. After that I'll rent a room at the motel while rebuilding."

"My door is always open. Don't forget that."

"I won't," Jesse promised. "Any word from Jolene?"

"She was holed up at her ranch with the paramedic. They're both fine."

"That's what I expected but it's still good to hear." Jesse glanced around the room.

"If you're looking for the pretty doctor, she isn't here," Mitch said.

Jesse met the man's gaze. "Just stopped in to see how she was doing," he said casually. He took another big bite of the sandwich and chewed.

"That's nice and friendly of you."

Jesse continued to chew his sandwich, ignoring the teasing gleam in Mitch's eyes. "I'm a nice guy."

"So I hear. Heck. Even Lurie attests to that, so it must be true."

"Must be." Jesse finished the sandwich, wadded up the plastic wrapping and tossed it in the wastebasket. He adopted a nonchalant attitude. "So where is Dr. Sherwood? Out on call?"

"She's gone."

"Gone?" Jesse no longer made any pretense of disinterest. "What do you mean she's gone?"

Seeing Jesse's face, Mitch became serious. "She left this morning to get a flight back to Courage Bay. Family emergency. Her aunt had an aneurysm. She's in the ICU."

Jesse silently digested the news. He expelled a breath.

"I'm sorry, Jesse."

Jesse schooled his expression. "Nothing to be sorry about." Without another word, he turned and walked out of the building.

She was gone.

AMY WAS SITTING in the chair beside her aunt's bed when Rachel knocked softly on the door. "Ian's here," she told her. "He's in the private room reserved for family members." She stepped inside as she spoke and checked Amy's aunt. As Amy already knew, there was no change.

Her son waited for her on one of the worn waiting-room chairs, looking much too serious for a thirteen-year-old. His legs and arms had the gangly length of adolescence and already he was an inch taller than her five feet six. He stood, shifted nervously as she came into the room. Suppressing the usual embarrassed protests, he allowed her to hug him hard. Her arms tightened around him. She found herself unable to let go. He began to squirm.

"Mom, you're choking me. Jeesh."

She loosened her hold and he wriggled out of her arms. She saw the sole hair on his chin that was his proud claim to impending manhood. She leaned in and kissed his cheek. "I missed you, honey."

"You've been gone two days, Mom." He rubbed his cheek.

She looked into her son's blue-green eyes, the same color as hers. That was where the resemblance ended. In looks and in the tall frame that would soon fill out, Ian was his father.

"It seems much longer, sweetie." She ruffled his hair. He rolled his eyes.

"Rachel says you're great with the baby."

He shrugged, but surrendered a half smile. "He's all right for a little rugrat."

She smiled, gestured toward the couch. "Let's sit a minute."

Her son's face sobered as he sat down.

"I'm sorry I wasn't here when Aunt Betts got sick," Amy said.

Ian shrugged. His gaze shifted from hers. "I wasn't there either. I was at Jeremy's."

"Aunt Betts wouldn't want either of us feeling guilty, you know that. Things happen in life sometimes and we have no control over them. Some things humans aren't able to prevent or change. Doctors, parents, we all have things we wish we could have prevented or done differently."

Her son's expression took on the long-suffering look he reserved for Amy's lectures. She paused, glanced around the room. It was empty, but fearing interruption, she gave him a small smile and touched his forearm. "Why don't we go down and see if Rachel's office is available?"

Her son's face became alert. "What is it, Mom? Is it Aunt Betts? Has she…" He couldn't finish.

"No, no." He allowed her to take both his hands in hers. She looked down. Such large hands for a young boy. She met his eyes. She had not expected this to be so hard. She wanted to be certain he understood. "Aunt Betts' condition is the same. But she suffered a major stroke, Ian. Machines are keeping her systems alive right now."

Ian blinked hard. She wanted to tell him he wasn't too big to cry. No one was too big to cry. But she knew it would only make him angrier.

"Aunt Betts would hate that," he said.

Her son was not so young after all. She nodded, proud of him. "You're right, Ian, she wouldn't like that.

He surprised her by squeezing her hands.

She took a silent breath. "Do you remember that time you asked me about your father? Your real father?"

Her son grew even more solemn.

"And I explained your father and I were never married, that we had been teenagers when we knew each other and were no longer together when I learned I was pregnant with you."

"You said he'd moved away a few months before you found out you were pregnant."

"And I tried to contact him at the last address I had for him but he was no longer there."

"And you didn't know where he went," Ian supplied in a toneless voice.

"That's right. I didn't. Until two days ago."

Ian's head jerked up. His eyes widened as he stared at his mother.

"I found your father in the town where I went to help out during the hurricane. He's the sheriff there."

Ian said nothing. He stared at her, stunned.

"Shortly after he'd moved away from Washington, he had a terrible accident. His own father was killed. Your father was almost killed too, trying to rescue him. At first, the doctors didn't believe he'd ever walk again. The trauma to his face required complete facial reconstruction to the point I didn't recognize him when I first saw him."

"Is he okay now?" Ian asked quietly.

"He favors his right side when he gets tired, and he's scarred from all the operations, but overall, he's fine. And very lucky to be alive."

"Does he know about me?"

"No, not yet. I wanted to make sure the time was right to tell him, not during the middle of a disaster. Then I had to leave so suddenly. He knows I have a son but he assumes you're Malcolm's child. He did try to contact me once about seven years ago, when he was better, but Malcolm answered the phone and told him he was my husband. He didn't try to contact me after that.

"But when the worst is over here and things have settled down, I'd like to tell him all about you. I know he'll want to meet you. And you'll want to meet him."

Her son angled his head to study her. "Did you love him, Mom?"

She smiled. "More than anyone else I'd ever loved in my life…until you came along."

He returned her smile before becoming serious again. "But you said you and he were no longer together when you found out you were pregnant with me."

"We were still dating when he moved away with his father. He even came back for my eighteenth birthday, promised he'd return to take me to the senior prom, but I never saw him again until two days ago. When he got back from visiting me, he learned his father had gotten a job in New Mexico. He was going to call me as soon as they got settled. Six days after I last saw him, the accident happened. He was afraid if he contacted me, told me the truth, I'd have gone to him, giving up my scholarship and my chance to be a doctor."

"Would you have?" Ian asked.

She nodded. "So he decided to keep the accident a secret."

"And all this time, you thought he'd dumped you."

She nodded.

"And you just learned the truth?"

She nodded again.

"Whoa. I bet you were pissed."

"Ian, language," she reprimanded, then smiled. "Royally."

"Are you still…*angry?*"

"No. I understand why he made the decision, and I'm grateful, but I still think I should have had the opportunity to make a choice in the situation." She ruffled his hair once more. "You know me. Control freak."

"Obviously my father knew it, too."

My father. The words spoken by her son echoed in the room. Ian was thoughtful for several moments. "When we talked about him before, you told me his name was Jesse Boone."

Amy nodded.

"Jesse Boone," Ian repeated, as if testing out the name. "He's a sheriff?"

"Real-life Texas sheriff. Hat, gun, badge, the whole enchilada. Only he drove a Bronco instead of riding the real thing. At least, he did before it got flattened by a tree during the storm."

Ian looked at her questioningly.

"Don't ask." She dismissed the dangerous escapade with a wave. Her son had enough to digest at the moment. He didn't need to know his mother had been caught in the middle of a hurricane.

"Mom?" Something in his voice reminded her he was still so very young.

"Yes, honey?"

He fidgeted in his seat. "Do you think he'll like me?"

Not caring he would blush, she pulled him into a tight embrace. "Oh, honey, he's going to love you." She felt her son hug her back.

After the embrace, Ian's face was grave again. "So, Aunt Betts is pretty bad?"

"I'm afraid so, honey. The doctors are doing everything they can. We'll just have to see what happens from there."

"She said she had a headache that morning. She said she'd go see the chiropractor, and he'd take care of her."

"Would you like to see her?"

Ian considered. "I think I'd like to remember her how she was."

"She'd like that." Amy patted his hands. "Grandma's coming in as soon as she can get a flight. She'll be here before the day's over."

Ian nodded. The furrows remained in his brow, and again, Amy thought he was much too young for such a heavy load.

"There's no sense you hanging around here. How 'bout I get Rachel to take you home?"

"You're not coming home yet?"

"I'm going to stay here a little while longer, talk with one of the neurosurgeons about Aunt Betts. Grandma will probably want to come here straight from the airport, then we'll come home." She fished in her purse for her wallet and gave several bills to Ian. "If we're late, order in pizza."

"Can Jeremy come over?"

"You know the rules. No friends over when there's no adult supervision." She stood.

"I'm thirteen, Mom," Ian coaxed as he got up from the couch.

She put her arms around his shoulders as they headed to the elevator. "I'll make it up to you."

"That new XBox game I've been waiting for was just released."

Her son gave her a smile. He'd be fine, Amy

thought. A little warier of life and its whims, but overall okay.

"We'll see," she answered. She pushed the elevator's down button.

"Hey, Mom?"

"Yes, honey?"

"Do you have any pictures of, you know…?"

"Your father?" she supplied, the idea still so new to Ian.

He nodded. She laid her hand on his cheek and turned his face toward the elevator door's metallic reflection. "His eyes are a much darker blue and he was four years older than you are when I met him, but otherwise, you're him."

Her son stared at his image until the doors parted. They stepped into the car. Amy said hello to the two nurses in the car and introduced her son.

When they got off, Amy said, "Of course, your father looks much different now. I didn't even recognize him at first. But there's a heart-shaped candy box in the bottom drawer of my dresser underneath a pile of clothes. There's some pictures of him in there."

They found Rachel in her office, the baby on her lap.

"Oh, Rachel, he's grown." One of the characteristics of Noonan's Syndrome was short stature. Heath also exhibited the downward slant, low nasal bridge and broad neck of individuals with the disorder. His motor functions were below average, but he grabbed the finger Amy offered him in a tight grip.

"He's beautiful," Amy told Rachel and Guy. Ian leaned over and tickled the child's chin. The baby gurgled with pleasure.

"Ian, my man." Guy, who had been standing nearby, beaming at his family, clasped his hand on the teenager's shoulder. "I'd say you're ready for learning the fine art of diaper-changing. What do you think, Amy?"

Ian's eyes widened. "Gross. Feeding him that disgusting green stuff is where I draw the line."

Guy grinned. "You mean the ground liver he used to blow raspberries at you."

Ian looked at the child. "I don't blame you, buddy. Somebody tried to feed that to me and I'd do the same thing."

"What are you telling us?" Rachel bounced the baby on her knee. "You're not up for any more adventures in baby-sitting?"

Ian shrugged, stroking the baby's downy hair. The child's hairline was low, another indication of the disease. "I don't mind hanging out with the little munchkin a little more. If it's okay with you guys?"

"We'd love to have you, Ian." Rachel stood and handed him the baby. "Here you go."

Ian wrapped his arms around Heath, protecting his head. The baby rested against his chest. Seeing him cradle an infant in his arms, Amy again was struck by the thought that soon her son would be a man.

She made arrangements with Rachel to call later and pick up Ian. After they left, she went back up to ICU to check on Aunt Betts. As she'd expected, there was no change. She looked again at her aunt, once-vibrant with her shock of red hair and penchant for chandelier earrings and anything purple, and was glad Ian had made the decision not to see her here now, her red hair gone, her body flat and lifeless in a faded blue hospital gown.

Amy found the operating neurosurgeon and discussed the case. She was happy to hear the swelling had gone down slightly, but the surgeon's cautious expression did not encourage her. After she finished talking to him, she used the hospital's computer to search medical databases for similar cases and conditions, hoping to find something, anything that could improve her aunt's chances. She knew it was highly unlikely, but she had to do something. Her review of similar cases only confirmed the inevitable, but she continued her search, loath to the alternative of sitting in ICU, staring at her aunt, feeling helpless. Soon the words began to blur. Besides catnaps caught here and there, she had not slept for any significant length of time in almost three days. When she found herself nodding off, she pushed herself away from the computer and headed to the cafeteria.

The cashier looked down at her cardboard cup. "Now that smells like coffee."

Amy smiled as she handed her the dollar bills. "One hundred percent Colombian, Irmela. Fourth one today."

The cashier leaned back slightly to give Amy a once-over. "Woo-wee. You leave us for two days and you come back a changed woman." She wriggled her eyebrows. "Something go down in that little Texas town that I should know about?"

Amy was able to muster a smile as she raised the coffee to her lips. She thought of Jesse for the thousandth time that day.

"You have no idea, Irmela."

CHAPTER THIRTEEN

SHE STARTED toward the door. "I'll see you later."

"Where you going, Doc?" the cashier called after her. "Leaving me high and dry without a single detail. Don't hold out on me now, girl. My shift doesn't end until six. You come on back later and fill me in."

Amy smiled until the elevator opened on the ICU floor. She went into her aunt's room, sat down in the chair next to the bed and sipped her coffee. When she'd finished, she threw the container in the garbage can and leaned back, resting her head along the edge of the chair, the hum of the machines almost soothing. She would close her eyes for only a few minutes.

When she awoke, the room was dim and her mother was shaking her gently.

"Mom." She became instantly awake. "How'd you get here? I thought you were going to call me so I could pick you up at the airport?"

"I didn't want to bother you, hon." Her mother's voice was hushed. "We rented a car at the airport." She gazed at her sister, her expression stricken. She turned to her daughter and opened her arms. "I need a big squeeze, sweetie."

Amy fell into her arms. Although she and her mother had had their differences while Amy was growing up, time and maturity had erased past conflicts and brought them closer.

Over her mother's shoulder, Amy saw an older, distinguished-looking man waiting in the hall.

"We?" she whispered in her mother's ear.

Her mother tipped her head back to see her daughter. "Glenn."

"Is that him in the hall?"

Her mother nodded, her cheeks the pink of a schoolgirl's. "Isn't he yummy?"

"Mom?" Amy leaned back and assessed her mother. "You're not wearing glasses."

"I got that new laser vision correction. It was like a miracle. A few minutes and I was seeing twenty-twenty."

"Yes, that's an amazing procedure. Your hair's different too. Lighter."

"Platinum sunsplash with foils. Took twenty years off me." She looked over her shoulder. With a coy smile, she waggled her fingers in a wave at the man. She turned back to her daughter. "He took twenty years off me."

"Mom!"

Her mother patted Amy's cheek. "We only live once, darling." She turned to the still figure on the bed, her arm still around her daughter's waist. "That's what Betts would say, wouldn't she?"

Amy had the sudden urge to rest her head on her mother's shoulder, but even as a child, she'd prided herself on being strong, invulnerable.

"Poor Betts," her mom said, staring at her sister. "It's funny. She was the older sister but I always thought of her as the younger of the two of us. She had such a zest for life." Her mother's arm tightened around Amy's waist. "She never had children. She told me once she would have regretted that decision if she hadn't had you and Ian come into her life. You were like a daughter to her."

"Ian and I wouldn't be where we are today if it wasn't for Aunt Betts."

Her mother faced her. "How bad is it, Doctor?"

Amy repeated all she had learned. "As soon as the swelling subsides, they'll stop the medication. Then we'll see if she wakes up."

Her mother didn't have to ask what happened next if she didn't. The machines keeping the woman in the bed alive hummed in the silence.

"What do you think?" her mother asked, her gaze fastened on her sister.

"I think we'll have to wait and see."

Her mother nodded. "Why don't you go on out and introduce yourself to Glenn. He knows all about you, of course. I never stop bragging. I'm just going to sit here a moment with Betts, catch her up on everything." She smiled bravely, although Amy saw the sheen of tears in her eyes.

"Sure, Mom." Amy glanced over her shoulder once more as she left the room to see her mother kneeling down by the bed as Amy had done only hours earlier, her hands folded in prayer.

"Hello." Amy extended her hand to the handsome gentleman in the hall. "I'm Peg's daughter, Amy."

"No introduction needed, miss." The man took her hand in a warm grip. "Glenn Mulligan. I'm sorry our meeting isn't under more pleasant circumstances. How is your aunt's condition?"

"Unchanged, I'm afraid. We're waiting to see if there's any response once the swelling subsides and the medication is discontinued, but…" Amy faltered.

Glenn patted her hand. "And in the meantime, we'll pray."

"Yes," Amy agreed, already liking this man with his kind eyes. "How did you and my mother meet?"

"She rear-ended me."

"Excuse me?" Amy asked.

"He loves to tell this story." Peg, her makeup streaked with tears, leaned against the doorway, a weak smile on her face.

Glenn sent her an encouraging wink. "Your mother drives like a madwoman, you know, Amy."

"Me?" Peg protested. "You're the one with the mid-life-crisis convertible." She moved next to Glenn. He put his arm around her and she leaned against him for support.

"It's red, too," Glenn added, giving Amy a wink now. "I wanted to buy your mother a matching one but she'd have none of it."

"And have everyone thinking I'm your trophy girlfriend," Peg said indignantly. "I don't think so."

Amy chuckled.

"You should hear the talk already at the Hair Gallery." Peg rolled her eyes.

"I can imagine," Amy sympathized.

A young nurse came by and nodded to the trio. "Excuse me. I'm just going to look in for a minute."

The group parted, fell silent as they watched the nurse check vitals, monitors.

"Excuse me." Amy left to confer with the nurse. She returned and tried to look optimistic as she faced her mother. "Well." She put her hands together. "You two are probably anxious to get unpacked and get settled. Are you hungry?"

"Don't worry none about us, Amy. You, my darling daughter, look like death warmed over. When was the last time you had a good night's sleep?"

Amy's hesitation was answer enough for her mother. "That's what I thought," Peg said with a knowing look at Glenn. "My girl, always trying to save the world."

When Amy started to protest, her mother raised a halting hand.

"No ifs, ands or buts. You need a home-cooked meal and a few hours sleep. Then we'll both come back and see how everything is. Deal?"

History had taught Amy it was useless to argue when her mother had made up her mind, so she relented with a nod.

"And Glenn can get to know my gorgeous grandson, Ian. Where is he by the way?"

"He was here earlier. He's staying at the house of two of my colleagues. I believe he's fallen in love."

Peg crossed her arms. "And how old is this little heartbreaker trying to get her claws into my grandson?"

Amy smiled. "Not even a year old. And it's a he, not a she."

"A baby?" Peg relaxed.

"You should see Ian with him."

"I'm ready. Let's go."

Amy stopped by the nurses' station to confirm they had all her contact numbers. She called Rachel from the car to let her know she was on her way to pick up Ian. She'd given her mother the house keys and told her to go on ahead. Amy would meet her and Glenn there after she picked up Ian.

As she drove Ian home, Amy could feel the mental and physical exhaustion of the last two days pulling her under. She fought back, drawing on the last remnants of her inner resources, but after a simple meal of grilled steaks, salad and baked potatoes, she succumbed to her mother's orders and lay down. It was dark when she woke. She glanced at the clock on the nightstand and saw it was two o'clock in the morning. She heard the low murmur of the television downstairs and went down to investigate. She found her mother, sipping from a coffee cup, watching an old black-and-white movie. Amy settled on the wide ottoman at the end of her mother's chair. "You should have wakened me."

"You needed your sleep. I checked in with the hospital. Nothing has changed. We'll go over first thing in the morning."

"What about you?" Amy asked. "Can't sleep?"

Her mother shrugged. "My body is beat but my mind is whirling."

"It's been a long day."

They silently watched the flickering images on the screen for a few minutes.

"See that actor. Dean Martin. That's who Glenn looks like, don't you think?"

Amy saw the resemblance. "Glenn is a handsome man." She turned back to her mother.

Her mother nodded. "I rear-ended his car because I was paying too much attention to looking at him. But don't you dare tell him that."

Amy drew an *X* over her heart. "You really like him."

Her mother rolled her eyes. "Falling in love at my age. Who'd have thought it? After all these years alone."

"I think it's great. And Glenn seems like a wonderful man."

With a contented smile, her mother raised her mug and took a sip. "How about you? It's been four years since your divorce from Malcolm. Anyone interesting in your life?"

Amy suppressed a strong urge to chew on a fingernail, knowing that would give her away immediately. She tucked her hands under her behind.

"Is there someone?" Her mother eyed her.

"You know I went to Texas, to a small town named Turning Point, to help out during the hurricane. I was there when I got the word about Aunt Betts."

"You met someone in Texas?" Peg leaned forward.

"Actually, I ran into someone I'd known before."

Peg frowned. "Who?"

Amy took a deep breath. "Jesse Boone."

Peg jerked back as if someone had slapped her. "Jesse Boone," she repeated softly. "After all these years. What the hell were the chances? What's he doing in Texas?"

"He's the sheriff."

Her mother's eyes widened. "Jesse Boone. A sheriff? Now that doesn't surprise me. Beneath that boy's wild ways, there always was a good heart."

"I thought you never liked Jesse."

"I didn't like him for you. There's a difference. Is he married?"

"No. Most eligible bachelor in three counties to hear the locals talk."

"So..." her mother started cautiously, "what happened when you saw each other? It's been how many years?"

"Fourteen."

"Fourteen years." Peg shook her head. "Does he look the same?" She studied her daughter, waiting for her response.

"Actually I didn't even know it was him at first. He had a horrible accident. Remember when he came up for my eighteenth birthday?"

"It was the last time you saw him."

"The accident happened shortly after. He was on the job with his father when a gas tank exploded. His father was killed instantly. Jesse was almost killed trying to save him. The trauma to his face required extensive reconstructive surgery. You wouldn't recognize him."

Her mother sat quietly for a few minutes. "Is he all right now?"

"All in all, his recovery is remarkable. At first, the

doctors didn't think he'd ever walk again. He'll never be the star quarterback he was in high school, but other than the scarring and a tendency to favor his right side when he gets tired, he's okay." Amy leaned in. "That's why he never contacted me after I saw him that last time. He said he was afraid I'd give up my scholarship, my schooling."

"You would have, you know."

"Probably. But I can't help but think that if he had really loved me, he would have trusted our love to find a way."

"Maybe it did," her mother said gently.

Amy considered. "Maybe. I just don't think he should have made the decision for me."

"You were eighteen, Amy. How could you have known what you wanted? You would have screwed up your life forever. Scraping by paycheck to paycheck in some dead-end job, taking care of a cripple."

Her mother had averted her gaze from Amy and was picking at a loose thread on the arm of the chair. Finally their eyes met.

"You knew," Amy said, an edge in her voice. "All this time, you knew what happened to him. You knew about the accident, his father's death. All these years, you let me think he'd abandoned me." Fury choked her voice.

Her mother sat very still, her hands folded in her lap, her face expressionless as she submitted to her daughter's accusations. She waited, allowing Amy to continue as if she owed her daughter that much. Amy was seething, but she had enough presence of mind not to speak further and say something in the heat of anger that she would regret later. After several silent seconds, her mother spoke.

"The hospital contacted me. He'd given them your name and number. I knew you would give up everything and go to him. I went to see him instead. I asked him to let you go, to give you the opportunity to go to school, become a doctor, make something of yourself. You had worked so hard for your scholarship."

Amy sat stone-faced.

"He agreed. I didn't know about the baby then. No one did until months later. By then, Jesse had been transferred to another hospital. Even if I could have found him, how were you going to go to med school with a baby and a crippled husband?"

Amy stood. "He had a right to know about his son. Just as I had a right to know about the accident. Damn it, Mom. Even I don't try to play God."

"I wasn't trying to play God. But I was your mother, and I did what I thought was best for you. So you told him about Ian?"

Amy exhaled a long breath. She sank back down onto the ottoman. "No. At first, I didn't know it was him, and then when I did find out, I was so angry. Then the hurricane struck and I got the radio call about Aunt Betts. I didn't even get a chance to say good-bye." She looked wearily at her mother. "You know, seven years ago he tried to call me."

"What happened?"

"Malcolm answered the phone."

Her mother's hand lifted slightly, then curled into a

ball as if she knew her daughter would not welcome her touch. Amy looked at her mother's fisted hand. Her hands had been taught to comfort, but they did not reach out now. Her mother's fear was justified.

"What are you going to do now?" Peg asked.

"I already told Ian about his father. All's left now is for me to tell Jesse about his son. It's not the kind of news I want to break over the phone though. As soon as I can, I'm going to fly to Texas."

"How'd Ian take the news?"

Amy smiled. "Pretty well considering. He's curious of course. I'm sure he's experiencing a lot of other emotions, but you know Ian. He's always been mature for his age."

"The little man of the house," her mother commented.

About to suggest to her mother that it could have been otherwise, Amy bit her tongue. Her anger was still too high, her emotions too raw.

"So, he didn't mention anything to you about his father tonight?" Amy asked.

Peg shook her head.

"Ian always keeps his cards close to his chest, but there have got to be some heavy-duty thoughts going on in that thirteen-year-old head of his right now."

"How do you think Jesse is going to react?"

"I don't know. When I discovered it was him in Texas, I ran through a whole range of emotions. Anger, confusion, joy. I imagine Jesse is about to have the same experience."

"He didn't tell you that I came to see him?"

Amy shook her head.

"I did what I thought was best for you."

Amy looked at her mother. Her hands lay twisted together in her lap. The nails were neat and well-shaped with the look of a professional manicure, but the knuckles were still knobby, the skin roughened from years of hard work.

"You can be mad at me if you want," Peg told her daughter, "but if I had to do it all over again, I would still make the same decision."

Amy stood. "It was not your decision to make."

"Shhh, you'll wake the household."

Amy felt her control slipping. The past two days were taking their toll. "Don't 'shhh' me. This is my house."

Her mother stood. "Glenn and I will leave in the morning. We'll go to a hotel."

"No." Amy dropped down onto the ottoman again. "No. That's not what I want." She felt her mother's hand, tentative, on her shoulder.

"What *do* you want, Amy?"

Amy didn't realize she was crying until she tasted the tears. "I want fourteen years."

Her mother stayed silent, standing by her daughter's side, her hand on her shoulder. She could not give Amy what she'd lost. No one could.

"Tomorrow is going to be another long day," Amy said, rising to her feet. "We should get some rest." She started toward the hall stairs.

"Amy?" Her mother's voice stopped her. "Do you still love him?"

She turned and faced her mother. "I never stopped."

THE DAYS that followed became a waiting game, a blur of bedside vigils, sleepless nights, a diet of coffee and convenience foods. Amy resumed her responsibilities at the hospital, grateful to have her mind occupied elsewhere for many hours. Otherwise she sat and thought of the recent days and wondered about the future. Aunt Betts' swelling subsided. All medications were stopped. Still there was no response. As a medical professional, Amy knew the decision should have been made before this. But in her heart, she prayed for more time. And a miracle.

There was no change.

The family gathered at the hospital. This time, knowing it would be the last time, Ian chose to come and say good-bye to Aunt Betts. Standing bravely by his mother's side, he hid his nervousness behind a poker face. Amy was again reminded of his father. Ian knelt beside the bed, and, folding his hands in prayer, he squeezed his eyes tight and silently said good-bye. He opened his eyes, stood, and looked at his mother. His features crumpled.

Amy took him in her arms and rocked him gently as he cried. Gradually, his shoulders stilled and he straightened, swiping the dampness off his face. She laid her hand on his cheek. "You are very lucky to have loved someone so much."

He turned away and went into the hall, embarrassed by his display of emotion. She followed him into the waiting room and sat beside him, taking his hand.

"You don't need to hold my hand," he said.

"No, I need you to hold mine."

They waited as Amy's mother said good-bye to her sister. She came out, leaning on Glenn's arm, looking older than Amy remembered.

"After the blessing, Grandma's going down to the hospital chapel," Amy told her son. "It would be good if you went with her."

Ian nodded. Father Allen from her aunt's church came to administer the last rites. When he finished, the small group stood by the bedside, hands still joined. There was only one thing left to be done. Amy looked at her mother. "I'll meet you in the chapel in a few minutes."

Her mother nodded. Amy fought back tears as Ian offered his grandmother his arm. Glenn took Peg's other arm and the trio walked toward the elevator. The elevator doors opened, closed. Amy was alone. She turned back to the hospital room.

She did not need to be here. Other hospital personnel could perform the process. But she had asked to be the one, and her request had been approved. Some would think her brave. Amy knew it was selfishness that brought her here to the foot of her aunt's bed. Only those in the medical profession could understand that what she was about to do would give her the comfort of at least being able to do something.

She pulled out the intravenous line bringing fluids. She shut down the oxygen, gently removed the ventilator tube. She turned down the dials, shut off the machines maintaining organ function. Her movements were brisk, efficient. She was a good doctor.

When she was done, she pulled a chair up to Aunt

Betts's bedside. She took her aunt's hands in hers and waited. She did not know how long she sat. She watched. The lines went flat.

She stood, still holding her aunt's hands. She leaned down and kissed her brow.

"I miss you already," she whispered.

Pressing the buzzer, she called the nurses. They would finish. She held her body very straight and still as she walked out of the room. One misstep, one stumble, and she would be finished.

She took the stairs down, avoiding the elevator and other people. Her breath was shallow, as if a great weight pressed against her chest. She reached the ground floor and stepped into the hospital lobby, stopping when she saw a tall figure moving through the automatic entrance doors. Surely it was her imagination, the oasis a lone survivor would perceive in the hot desert sun.

Jesse stopped when he saw her. Then his steps quickened. Her shoulders fell as she walked slowly into his arms. His large body curved like a sail around her slight figure, and she pressed herself to him as if she could not get close enough.

"It seems," he said in a low voice near her ear, "we have this habit of not saying good-bye to each other."

Amy didn't think she had any tears left. She was wrong.

He let her cry. She clutched his shirtfront, afraid that if she let go, he'd vanish before her eyes. He stroked her back, her hair, murmured soothing sounds. She leaned into him and cried harder. It was easily a full ten minutes before she could compose herself enough to look up into his face, once strange, now becoming familiar to her. She remembered she was in the hospital lobby in full display of colleagues and staff, but she didn't care. She was in Jesse's arms again. At that moment, that was all that mattered.

"I'm so glad you came. Thank you."

His knuckle softly brushed away a tear on her cheek. "I would have come sooner, but the hurricane—"

She shook her head, stopping him. "I wanted to stay longer, be there to help out."

"You were needed here, Amy. You had to go."

"Everything happened so fast. There was no time to try and reach you, let you know I had to leave." She looked up into his eyes. "I'm glad you're here."

His fingers moved softly against her skin. "I missed you." He bent his head, gently brushing his lips against hers in a slow, sweet kiss.

Amy's arms tightened around him involuntarily. *Don't go,* she thought. *Don't leave me this time.*

"Mom?"

Amy jerked away from Jesse, breaking the embrace. She watched his eyes grow puzzled as her own pleaded. His gaze moved past her. He stepped back with a stagger as if punched squarely on the jaw. Muscles frozen, lips slightly parted, he looked at his son for the first time.

CHAPTER FOURTEEN

"MOM?"

Jesse's gaze remained fixed on Ian as the boy walked toward them, the image of Jesse nineteen years ago. Confusion clouded Jesse's eyes as Ian stood beside Amy, taller than his mother. Amy looped her arm around his waist. "Hi, honey."

The boy stared back at Jesse with equal curiosity. Jesse swallowed dryly. His gaze still on the boy, he said to Amy, "This is your son?"

Our son, she corrected silently. Jesse's gaze darted to her. She nodded. His eyes darkened.

"This is Ian," she said. "Ian, this is Jesse Boone."

The man and boy faced each other. Neither spoke. Amy felt the tension in her son's body. The silence stretched out. Jesse's gaze stayed locked on the boy. Amy was about to tell him the truth when Jesse took a step forward and extended his hand. "Hello, Ian."

The boy hesitated before he took his father's hand.

"It's good to meet you, Ian." Jesse said the name again, as if trying to get used to it.

The boy looked squarely into the man's face.

"Thank you for coming, sir." Amy was never more proud of her son than at that moment.

"I'm glad I came. I only wish…" Jesse swallowed. "I'd come sooner." He released the boy's hand and stepped back. His expression changed as his gaze shifted to Amy.

Peg and Glenn joined the group. Peg looked at Jesse, glanced at her daughter curiously.

"Mom, it's Jesse," Amy told her.

A confusion similar to Jesse's only minutes earlier crossed her mother's features, but as she took in the man, her expression softened. "Hello, Jesse."

"Mrs. Sherwood." The same warmth was not offered in his greeting. Amy saw anger flare in his eyes. So did her mother.

"It was good of you to come," Peg said.

"I'm glad I did." His voice remained reserved, although Amy had no doubt his answer was sincere.

"This is my friend, Glenn Mulligan."

The two men shook hands.

Peg put her arm around her grandson almost possessively. "Amy, Glenn and I will take Ian back to the house. We'll see you both there?" Her gaze flickered to Jesse.

Amy looked at Jesse. His gaze went to their son, then back to her. He nodded.

"Grandma and Glenn will take you home and we'll be right behind you," Amy said. "Okay, Ian?"

Ian shrugged. "Sure."

The trio headed toward the exit. As the automatic doors parted, Ian glanced over his shoulder. Jesse's gaze had not left the boy. They looked at each other. Jesse smiled, lifted his hand good-bye. Ian turned without response.

Jesse turned to her, his expression stony, the man she had met that first morning in Turning Point.

"This is not how I wanted you to find out."

He raised a palm, halting her explanation. "Not here," he said. "Someplace private."

She led him outside to a bench at the side of the hospital, several feet from any others. They sat down. Jesse stared ahead unseeingly.

"Jesus," he said finally.

He fisted his hand and slammed it against the seat, shattering the uneasy silence. "You should have told me."

"I was going to."

"When?"

"At first, I was so angry with you, then I had to come to terms with the fact that I had found you after all these years. The storm came, the news of Aunt Betts. I had to go."

"You had plenty of opportunity." His voice was hard.

"So did you," she snapped back. "I don't want to do this, Jesse."

For several moments, neither of them spoke. When Jesse finally did, his voice was eerily calm. "Fourteen years ago, I made my decision. Never once did I doubt it was the wrong choice." He paused. "Until now."

Amy raised her hand, then hesitated, as her mother had only last night. She knew her touch would not be welcome.

"Did your mother really despise me that much?" Jesse's voice was tired.

"She didn't know I was pregnant when she went to see you. No one did for several months. I'd always been irregular. After you left, I wasn't eating right, losing weight. I tried to blame the missed periods on that. When I finally had to consider the fact it could be something else, I was already in California in my first semester of college. I was so scared, I didn't even tell my mother until Thanksgiving break."

"I can imagine her reaction," Jesse said.

"She was angry at first. Disappointed too, but then she was actually very supportive." Some of the anger Amy had felt last night after she had learned what her mother had done began to dissolve. "She asked me what I wanted to do, if I had considered all the options."

"Had you?" Jesse asked quietly.

"Abortion—no, never. Adoption, yes. I thought about it, but I knew I would keep the child, no matter what the cost. It was our child. It was all I had left of you." She saw the pain etch new lines on his face. She had known they could never get back the fourteen years they'd lost. Now she feared they could never overcome them.

"My mother offered to take care of the baby after the birth until I finished medical school, but this child was my responsibility. Fortunately, Aunt Betts insisted I live with her and let her help with the child. I couldn't have made it without her." She paused, fresh grief welling inside her.

"I should have been there." Jesse rubbed his brow, anguish in his voice.

"Don't you see? That's how I felt when you first told me about your accident. All that time, I thought you had abandoned me, but I was the one who had abandoned you."

"You didn't know about the accident."

"You didn't know about the pregnancy," she countered. "After my mother learned about the pregnancy, she did try to find you, but you had been transferred from that hospital to another, then another. The paperwork had been misplaced or forwarded so many times, no one was certain where you were.

"Last night she also told me that you had tried to contact me after the accident, that she went to you in the hospital and begged you not to try to contact me again. You didn't tell me that." She tried not to make her voice accusatory.

"Your mother did come to me, but I was the one who made the final decision." He paused. "If I had known…" His voice trailed away.

Amy did not know what else to say, who was right, who was wrong. There were no answers.

"The first time I saw you was Tuesday afternoon, two thirty-five, October eighth, 1991, in the school library." Jesse spoke softly, breaking the silence. "Coach said he'd gotten me a tutor and I should sit tight and take in every word you said if I wanted to continue the season. You came into that library, all serious, your hips swaying, a stack of books pressed against your chest and an expression on your face that said 'Prepare to do battle.' I thought hell's bells, this one is going to be a handful."

The tiniest smile graced Amy's face. "Scared you, did I?"

"I never knew what the hell hit me. That day you wrote your name and phone number on a piece of looseleaf paper, told me not to lose it. The nurses found that piece of paper in my wallet when the hospital was looking for next of kin. One of the nurses asked me if you should be contacted. I nodded yes. The nurse spoke with your mother. She came to see me and I agreed to leave you alone. Still I kept that piece of paper for the longest time. I knew I was being foolish, but I couldn't seem to throw it away." He sighed as if wondering, like her, if too many years and too many secrets had destroyed their chances.

"So when did you finally throw it away?" Amy asked.

Jesse reached into his pants pocket and pulled out a worn sheet of paper. He opened it carefully so he wouldn't rip the creases, thin with years of folding and unfolding. He smoothed his hand across it. Amy saw her name written in her youthful, round, curvy script. Beneath it was her phone number.

"I didn't. I had a small metal file box at home for all my important papers. I kept it in there. I found the box in the rubble at my place. It survived the storm."

Amy stared at the sheet of paper with the fat cursive letters. "Just like us."

Jesse folded the paper, his face unreadable, and slid it back into his pocket.

"What do we do now, Jesse?"

He looked at her, the mask cracking, revealing the pain and uncertainty Amy shared.

"I don't know."

Her heart broke. "Are you going to stay?"

He nodded. "Yes. I'd like to spend time with Ian."

"That would be good. You can stay at the house if you like. There's room."

He shook his head. "No, I'll get a room at a motel. It would be easier."

"Of course." She adopted a polite manner. "How long can you stay?"

"I was planning on two days at the most."

There was never enough time for them.

"I have to get back to Turning Point," he said. "There's a lot to be done. But now that I know about Ian..." He rubbed his brow again, looked past her. "Everything's changed."

"Yes," Amy agreed. "Everything has changed. For all of us."

It seemed as if he wanted to say something more, but he remained silent. After several seconds, he stood. "You probably need to get back."

"Do you have a car?" she asked, getting up also.

He nodded. "I rented one at the airport."

"You can follow me to the house, or if you want to get a room first, I can write directions to my place from the motel."

"I'll get a room, then come over, if that's all right?" They were so formal they could have been two strangers.

"That's fine." She took out a notepad, wrote down the address, then handed him the sheet of paper. "Here. Don't lose it."

He smiled slightly as he folded the paper. Amy couldn't suppress the hope that sparked in her.

By the time she left the hospital and arrived home, the food and the phone calls of support and condolences had begun to come in. Peg was in the kitchen on the phone. Glenn was at the front door accepting a fruit basket delivery. Amy went to the refrigerator and took out a bottle of water as she listened to her mother thank the person on the other end for calling.

When Peg hung up, she looked at her daughter "Where's Jesse?"

"He went to get a motel room, then he'll be over. I gave him directions."

"How did he take everything?"

Amy shook her head. "I should have told him about Ian right away—when I found out it was really him."

"He's pretty angry?" Peg asked.

"Angry, confused. He's got a right to be. He lost fourteen years."

"So did you. So did Ian," her mother noted. "Is that reason enough to lose even more?"

"I can't answer that. And I can't answer for Jesse, either. How's Ian?"

"He was quiet on the way home. He's upstairs in his bedroom now, playing a video game."

Amy set the water bottle on the counter. "I think I'll go talk to him."

"Amy?" Her mother moved toward the sink, picked up some lettuce leaves and rinsed them under the faucet. "About everything...well, I did what I thought was right."

"I think that's what we all did, Mom. Except now everything is all wrong."

Ian lay on his stomach on his bed, furiously pushing the buttons on the video game controller.

"Hi, handsome," Amy said as she walked into the room and sat down on the bed beside him.

"Aw-w-w, Mom. You're not going to get all sappy on me, are you?"

"I might." She ruffled his hair. He ducked his head, his eyes never leaving the video screen while his fingers fought imaginary enemies.

"It's been quite a day, hasn't it, honey?"

"Yeah." Ian pressed a button. An alien got zapped on the screen.

"What did you think of Jesse?"

Ian shrugged. "He's big." He glanced up at his mother. "Do you think I'll get that tall?"

"From the looks of you already, I'd say yes."

Ian returned to his game. "He doesn't look anything like his pictures."

"I told you he wouldn't."

He glanced up at her again. "What did he think of me?"

"He was surprised."

"I'll bet."

"He's staying for two days. He'd like to spend as much time as possible with you, get to know you. Would that be okay?"

"I guess."

"It will probably be a little strange at first, but with time, I bet you and he will be just fine with each other."

Ian paused the video game and looked up at his mother. "Am I supposed to call him Dad or what?"

"You two will figure that out." Amy stood. "He's coming over as soon as he gets settled at the motel. He'll probably stay for dinner."

"Whatever." Ian started the video game again. Amy leaned down and kissed the top of his head.

"C'mon, Mom, cut it out."

"I don't want you playing that thing all day either." She gave her customary warning as she left the room and went downstairs.

Peg was cutting up tomatoes at the sink, while Glenn was peeling cucumbers at the table. "Glenn, I can do that," Amy told him.

"Don't start spoiling him on me, Amy," Peg warned.

Glenn smiled. "I'm glad to help out, Amy."

"He's a pretty good cook, too," Peg added, smiling at him. She turned to Amy. "How's Ian?"

"He told me not to get all sappy on him."

"Sounds like he'll be fine." Peg sounded relieved.

"He's not saying much at the moment."

"It's going to take time for all of you. You look tired, honey. Why don't you go take a nice, long hot bath and get yourself fixed up for dinner?"

Amy looked at Glenn. "She's not very subtle, is she?"

"That's our gal," Glenn said.

"Go now," Peg urged her. "Glenn and I will get dinner ready. I'd rather stay busy anyway."

Her mother turned back to the sink. Aunt Betts and her mother had never been close. Besides the large age difference between them, Amy suspected there had been some jealousy on her mother's part over Amy and Ian's close relationship with Betts. Still, her mother had just lost her only sister.

Amy went to Peg, put her arm around her shoulders and gave her a squeeze. "Thanks, Mom. I'll do cleanup."

"It's a deal. Off with you now." Her mother's eyes with their newly corrected vision became glassy.

Amy squeezed her shoulders again and gave her a kiss on the cheek. "I love you, Mom."

Peg blinked back her tears and smiled at her daughter. "Don't go getting all sappy on me, Amy."

Less than a half hour later, Amy was heading back downstairs. She had cut her bath short when her tears had come. As she walked toward the staircase, she heard voices coming from Ian's bedroom. She moved toward the room. From the doorway, she saw Jesse sitting on the end of the bed beside Ian, their brows furrowed, their bodies weaving and bobbing as they focused on playing the game on the video screen.

"You ever play NFL Fever?" Jesse asked.

"Yeah, but I like Madden 2005 better."

Amy stayed in the hall where she could watch them without interrupting them. Her son let out a triumphant whoop at a victory. Jesse's intense gaze stayed on the screen, but a small smile curled his lips. He glanced at Ian and Amy saw in his eyes the same wonder she had so often known. Her eyes filled with tears, but she didn't even try to stop them this time. She'd spent these past days praying for a miracle. She'd thought her prayers had gone unanswered, but she'd been wrong. She slipped away from the doorway.

Jesse cast a sidelong look at the boy beside him. Ian's gaze was glued to the screen. His body shifted, twisting in the same direction as the controller he wielded like a weapon. His features were still soft with youth, but the thinnest shadow of hair over his top lip predicted manhood.

"My cousin back in Texas has a couple of nephews around your age. One's a little older."

"Yeah?" Ian concentrated on the game.

"Their father lives out here in California."

Ian said nothing.

"My father was killed when I was eighteen. That was fourteen years ago."

Ian didn't respond. They played the game for a few minutes.

"My mom said you didn't know about me," Ian said without looking at him.

Jesse set down his controller. "No, I didn't. I didn't know I had a son until today."

Ian kept his gaze on the screen. "My mom was married for a while."

"I know. To Malcolm."

"He was my stepdad."

"Your mother told me you and he are still good buddies."

"That's right." Ian's fingers flew on the controller's buttons. "Most of the time though, I never had a father."

Jesse smiled. "I've never had a son. But there were lots of times I wished I did."

Ian glanced at him before returning his attention to the screen. "You never married?"

"No."

"Why?"

"I only met one person in my life I ever wanted to marry."

Ian turned to consider him. "My mother?"

"That's right."

"You loved her?"

Jesse nodded.

"You going to ask her to marry you?"

Jesse sat back. "I'm not sure what I'm going to do."

Ian returned to his game. "Thought you loved her."

"It's not that simple, Ian."

"She'd probably say no anyway."

"What if she didn't?"

Ian gave him a half-lidded look. "What do you mean?"

"What if I asked her to marry me and she said yes. Would you be okay with that?"

"Would I have to move to Texas?"

"That's where I live."

"I live here. I've got friends here."

"Texas is nice."

Ian turned off the video game, picked up the television's remote control and switched on the sports channel. "I like California."

"It would be nice to all be together."

Ian looked at him, one eyebrow raised. "My mom and I have been doing fine."

"I know. I'm glad you had each other, but I'd like to be part of your lives also." When Ian was silent, Jesse continued. "I'm not quite sure what is going to happen,

Ian, but I do know now that I've found you both, I'm not losing either of you again."

Ian stared at the television. Jesse sat beside him, feeling helpless.

"You like the Houston Astros?" Ian asked, not looking at him.

"Sure do. How 'bout you?"

"I'm a Dodgers man myself."

Jesse suppressed a smile. "Your mother mentioned that to me once."

Peg's voice sounded from downstairs. "Boys, dinner's ready."

Jesse stood. "Guess we better go."

Ian sighed as he clicked off the television and dragged himself off the bed. He looked Jesse squarely in the eye. "You ask my mother to marry you," he said grudgingly, "she probably won't say no."

"And what do you think if she does say yes?"

Ian shrugged. "The Texas part doesn't thrill me."

It wasn't much, but it was a beginning, Jesse thought. He'd take it.

"C'mon," Ian told him. "We gotta wash up before dinner. Mom has a thing about germs."

"Don't all moms?" Jesse said as he and his son started out of the room.

CHAPTER FIFTEEN

AUNT BETTS's funeral was two days later. As with most things in her life, Betts had not wanted a conventional funeral. She had participated wholeheartedly in every one of the church's charity functions, often organizing them single-handedly, but she attended church services sporadically and vocally expressed her opinions on what she deemed some of the more archaic rituals and rites. Her diatribes often included wakes and funerals designed to "wring the life out of a person until the deceased one looks the most animated person there."

To that end, she had left specific instructions on how she was to be laid to rest. A jazz band was to be hired and the dining room at the Courage Bay Bar and Grill rented. Everyone was to eat and dance and drink until they were drunk enough to dance down Courage Bay's streets and up into the mountains to scatter her ashes so she could always look down on the town she loved so much. As was her wish, Aunt Betts was laid to rest high above Courage Bay with laughter, song and celebration.

Still, the day was not without moments of tears, shared memories and the realization that life, no matter how full, was too damn short. Jesse's visit, too, was coming to an end. He was needed in Turning Point. His flight left that evening.

"Thank you again for coming," Amy told him as they walked through the terminal. "It meant a lot to me that you were here."

She had followed him to the airport to see him off. He had returned his rental car and they were heading to the check-in area. They'd invited Ian to go to the airport also, but with an insight beyond his young years, he had declined, granting Amy and Jesse a much-needed private good-bye. They'd had little opportunity to discuss the future. Amy sensed they had both skirted around the issue, still uncertain if two lives so separate could be merged without sacrifice.

"Your aunt seemed like a great lady," Jesse said.

"She was wonderful." Already Courage Bay seemed changed without Aunt Betts. "This place isn't going to be the same for me without her."

"How about Ian? He was pretty quiet today."

"He'll be okay. We'll both be okay. It takes time." She flashed a brave smile.

They reached the check-in counter. Jesse's flight would leave in forty minutes. Boarding began in twenty. Jesse and Amy sat down in seats along the wall.

"I wish I could stay longer but I've got to get back. Turning Point is still such a mess." He surprised her by grabbing her hand in a tight grasp.

For a moment, Amy could not find her voice.

"I know," she said at last. "They need you there. I'm grateful you could come for the short time you did."

She squeezed his hand. "Next time you'll stay longer. And as soon as my schedule permits, Ian and I will come see you."

"I'd like to have Ian spend some time with me in Turning Point. Maybe over school vacations?"

When the time had come for Jesse to say good-bye to Ian, they'd stood awkwardly facing each other. Jesse had handed Ian his card, every possible contact number scribbled on it. "Any time you need anything or just want to talk or anything at all, you call me."

Ian had nodded as he took the card. He'd swallowed, his Adam's apple bobbing in his long throat.

"And I'm going to be calling you and your mom on a regular basis, checking in, okay?"

"Yes, sir." Ian had turned the card over and over in his hands.

"No need for 'sirs,' son." The endearment, a common term, now had new meaning. "'Jesse' is just fine."

"Okay. Jesse."

Jesse had smiled at the boy and held out his hand. Jesse clasped Ian's shoulder as the two shook. "I'm so glad we got to meet."

"Me too, sir—I mean, Jesse."

"Okay then."

Neither had moved. Ian had swallowed. "You know how you said you never had a son but you thought about it sometimes and figured it would be great?"

Jesse had nodded.

"Sometimes I used to think about having a dad and thought it would be okay, too."

It had been Jesse's turn to swallow hard.

Now in the airport terminal, Amy looked at her son's father. "Ian would like that."

"You wouldn't mind?"

"No, I want you two to spend as much time as you can together. It will be good for you both."

They sat silently a few minutes, watching the passengers coming and going. Jesse would not let go of her hand. He cleared his throat. "Amy?"

She turned to him.

"I don't know—"

She pressed a finger to his lips, stopping him. "Neither do I, Jesse. Everything has happened so fast. There's still so much to figure out. We'll take it slow, step by step, and see what happens. We found each other again. You know about your son. I know what happened fourteen years ago when you vanished from my life. It's a good starting point. Let's take it slow and see what unfolds."

"After all these years." Jesse smiled. "Still the sensible one."

"Not always." She leaned in and kissed his lips. He clutched her shoulders, pulling her to him, deepening the kiss until she was dizzy.

When it ended, she dropped her forehead against his chest, missing him already. She inhaled the clean, soap-fresh scent of him, blindly traced his muscles with her fingertips, knowing this would have to last her until the next time they could be together. He kissed her hair, cupped her chin, lifted her face to him, kissed her cheeks, her nose, each eye closed, found her mouth once more and drank of her deeply like a desperate man. When finally he released her, she was trembling. Her emotions were too strong, threatening to embarrass her, and she breathed in deeply, struggling for composure. She looked at the watch on her wrist. "They'll be boarding."

He nodded, expelled a sigh. "Yes, I have to go."

Neither moved. Finally she nudged him and smiled playfully.

He chuckled softly. "Pathetic, aren't we?"

She stood, forcing herself to be steady, and reached out her hand. "Come on, I'll walk with you to the security check-in."

He took her hand and rose to his feet, slinging his travel bag over his shoulder. They stopped a few steps from the metal detectors. He looked at her, his expression cutting through her fragile resolve to be strong, adult and sensible.

"I have to go." He held her hand, his thumb moving softly against her skin.

"Yes, you do." Her voice faltered. She gave him a tiny smile. In the long silence that stretched between them, she feared she would begin to cry.

She brought her hand to his face and touched his cheek. "Kiss me quick and then go."

He kissed her long instead, again and again, soft and tender, fourteen years dissolving into this moment.

It was she who finally broke the embrace, pushing him gently but firmly away. She looked up into his eyes for the last time. "Go."

He ran his thumb across her lower lip as if to wipe away the taste of him. He turned. She watched him put his bag on the conveyer belt, step through the circle of metal detectors. He did not look back. A few steps and then he was gone.

"Stay," she whispered.

She was in the parking lot when she heard rapid, running steps behind her. A hand clamped down on her shoulder, startling her, turning her around.

"Jesse? What is it? What's wrong?"

He was gasping, struggling for breath. "I wanted to do it right this time, Amy. Not make any mistakes. Give us the long, slow courtship we missed. Dinner dates, flowers, weekends away, take the time to get to know each other all over again." He rubbed his forehead.

Amy waited, too surprised to speak.

"But hell, Amy, I'm afraid if I get on that flight and you walk out this door, I might never see you again."

She opened her mouth to reassure him that wasn't going to happen and found she couldn't. Because it had happened before.

"At eighteen, I believed we had a whole lifetime to be together, that nothing or no one could tear us apart," Jesse continued. "I know better now. I know if God has blessed me with a second chance with you, I damn well better not turn my back on it. We've already lost fourteen years. I don't want to lose a minute more. I've done a lot of thinking the past two days, Amy. What we do with that chance is up to us. What I don't know is if I'm right or wrong or coming or going."

He took her hands in his. "All I know is I love you and I believe you love me. The first time I lost you damn near killed me. I'm not taking any chances on losing you a second time."

He got down on one knee.

"Marry me, Amy."

She stared down at him, still stunned.

"It doesn't have to be today or tomorrow or even next week. Or it can be."

She smiled.

"I know this is all sudden. Hell, sometimes I still feel like I'm swept up in that damn hurricane again that turned everything in its path upside-down and inside-out. I'm not asking you and Ian to pack up and head out to Texas with me tonight. Ian already told me he's not thrilled with the idea of Texas. I can come here. I'll go anywhere you and Ian are, Amy, as long as we're together. I'll wait until you're ready and Ian's ready. You tell me when, but for today, just tell me." He took a long, deep breath. "Tell me you'll marry me."

She knelt down in front of him.

"Yes."

He stood and drew her up into his embrace, kissing her with passion and promise. She kissed him back, unashamed to cling to him and hold on too tight. He lifted his head to look deeply into her eyes.

"Yes?" he asked.

She laughed as she cupped his face in her hands. "I've waited since I was eighteen years old to be your wife, Jesse Boone. I'm not going to say no now."

They were still laughing, holding hands as they opened the back door and came into the house. The noise brought Peg into the kitchen.

"What in tarnation? Jesse, what are you still doing here?" She eyed the couple. A smile slowly curved her lips.

"We'll explain in a minute. Where's Ian?" Jesse crossed the kitchen, pulling Amy with him.

"In his bedroom. Where else? Why?"

"I've got a question to ask him," Jesse told her as he and Amy started down the hall.

Ian's bedroom door stood open. Jesse knocked lightly on the doorjamb. Ian looked up from the end of the bed where he was playing a handheld video game. "What are you doing here?" he blurted.

Jesse stopped short, for the first time uncertain.

"Did you miss your plane?" Ian eyed his mother's hand in Jesse's. "I told you Mom drives like an old lady."

"I did miss my plane, but it was my fault." Releasing Amy's hand, Jesse walked into the bedroom. "I needed to come back here to ask you a question." He squatted down in front of Ian, his expression solemn as he gazed at his son.

"A question?" Ian warily eyed the man across from him.

Jesse nodded.

The boy shrugged. "Sure, whatever."

Jesse took a deep breath. "We've talked about how I feel about your mother and how she feels about me. I also told you I can't think of anything that would give me greater happiness than for us to all be together one day. I know that day won't be tomorrow or next Tuesday or maybe not even until next year, but I'm hoping that day is sooner than later."

"What's the question?" Ian demanded.

"When the day does come, I'd like to know you share our decision to become a family. I'd like to ask you if you'd give me permission to marry your mother?"

Ian stared at his father. "Don't ya think you should ask her first?"

"I did."

"Oh, yeah?" Ian's voice turned hostile. "What did she say?"

Amy stepped into the room and sat down beside her son. "I said yes, Ian."

He tipped his head up to look at her sullenly. "Then what's everybody asking me for?"

"Because that's how families work, Ian," Jesse said. "They don't make decisions that will affect all the other members without talking to them about it."

"We're not your family," Ian shot back.

"You're my son. My blood."

"That doesn't make you a father."

"Ian—" Amy interrupted, but Jesse held up a palm to stop her.

"No, but I want to be your father. And I want to marry your mother. More than anything in the world, I want us to be a family."

"You guys are going to do what you want anyway," Ian grumbled. "It doesn't matter what I think."

"Your mother and I wouldn't deliberately do anything to make you unhappy."

"What about Texas?" Ian demanded.

"I told your mother if you and she didn't want to leave California, I would come here."

Ian eyes him suspiciously. "You're just saying that."

"I know you don't know me very well, Ian, but when you do, you'll know I don't say things I don't mean."

"There's a terrible need for medical services where Jesse lives, Ian. You and I have often discussed the possibility that once I finish my residency, I might go to work somewhere else besides Courage Bay."

"We haven't made any definite decisions yet, Ian," Jesse said, "except for the fact your mother and I would like us all to be together and want to find a way to make that work so everybody is happy."

Ian looked down at the small screen of his video game but didn't turn it on. He sighed. Jesse glanced at Amy. They waited. Ian sighed again.

"You don't have to give us an answer right now, Ian," Jesse told him. He glanced again at Amy for approval. She gave a slight nod. "Take some time to think about it. Like I said, everything has happened so fast, your mother and I aren't going to do anything right away either. We just wanted you to know what we hope will happen in the future. So—" Jesse stood to go. Amy rose from the bed.

They were almost to the hall when Ian said, "Grandma told me what she did." Jesse and Amy stopped and turned to the bed.

"She told me how the hospital called and she went there and asked you to stay away from Mom." He looked at Jesse. "She said she did it because she thought it was the best thing for Mom, but now she's not sure it was."

Amy sat down beside her son.

"I don't know if I want to go to Texas. I don't know what I want." He sighed. Amy put her hand on his knobby shoulder. Ian looked at Jesse. "But you marrying Mom, I think that would be the best thing for her."

"What about you, Ian?" Jesse asked his son.

The boy shrugged. "It'd be okay."

Amy smiled at her son. She threw her arms around him and pulled him to her.

"Mom," he protested, trying to wiggle out of her embrace, but she wouldn't let him go. She kept her arm around her son's shoulders as she reached out her hand to Jesse. He held it tight. Amy knew they would not let go of each other, either. Never again.

That was how Amy's mother, unable to put off her curiosity any longer, found them. Smiling, holding on tight. Together.

EPILOGUE

AMY ROCKED on the porch, looking out at the surrounding lands, waiting for the new Bronco with the star on its side to come over the horizon. Turning Point's landscape had changed. There were gaping holes where trees had been ripped out by the roots, open spaces where once a house or business stood. Reminders of Damon's wrath. Not that people were likely to forget. Yet they were getting on with their lives, rebuilding with the same stubborn determination that had created this town.

Amy gave a small yawn and stretched. She had finished her twelve-hour shift earlier that day and driven the distance from Beeville, where she was finishing her residency. After it was completed, she would take over Doc Holland's practice. As Mitch had predicted, Turning Point's doctor was ready to retire. In the meantime, Cheryl Tierney was working with him and studying for her nurse practitioner's license. Together she and Amy hoped to set up a new urgent care medical facility, which would help to relieve the area's sorely lacking medical emergency services. She and Jesse often got together with Cheryl and Noah Arkin, Turning Point's veterinarian. Noah had saved Cheryl's life during the hurricane when he'd pulled her out of a car caught in the river's violent current, and then captured her heart.

Nate Kellison, the paramedic who'd come with the Courage Bay team during Damon, was here in Turning Point, too, but Amy didn't see him as much. He was busy running the ranch with Jolene Angel and anxiously awaiting the birth of her baby. His new boss and future father-in-law, Mitch, also kept him busy working for the town's fire department.

Dana Ivie was here, too. Having finally met her match in pilot Micky Flynn, she'd found she couldn't just walk away. And neither could Micky, whose past relationships with women had strictly adhered to his be-gone-by-breakfast rule.

Amy saw the Bronco come into sight over the slight rise and smiled. The vehicle parked. She watched Jesse emerge, and walk toward the porch, never failing to enjoy his easy gait, the large, long frame of his body. *Her husband.* Her mind would tell her that again and again, and still it did not fail to amaze her.

They had decided if Ian agreed to live in Texas, he and Amy would move there before the school year started so Ian wouldn't have to change schools midyear. Ian had agreed, reluctantly, but once he arrived in Texas, Jesse's cousin's boys and the rest of Jesse's family took him as one of their own. Spending time together on a daily basis had also cemented his relationship with Jesse, and although there had been bumps along the way, the two were steadily progressing toward the closeness shared by a father and son. Ian's complaints were now fewer and pertained more to chores and bedtime curfews.

With Ian's blessing, Amy and Jesse had married last weekend in a simple ceremony on the land where his house had been rebuilt with friends throughout the community. Ian had been the best man.

Rachel had flown in with Guy and the baby to be Amy's maid of honor, and in an unconventional twist that surely would have pleased Aunt Betts, Amy had asked her mother to walk her down the aisle and give her away.

Jesse climbed the steps to the porch. She lifted her face for his kiss as he came to her. Her brow furrowed slightly as she looked past him. "Where's Ian?"

Jesse sat down in the rocking chair beside Amy. He took her hand as he began to rock, and kissed her fingertips.

"Aunt Edna asked if he could have dinner and sleep over with the boys."

"Again?" Amy chuckled softly. "I thought it was our turn for the sleepover."

"Probably, but Aunt Edna enjoys fussing over them. And—" he pulled her up by her hand and led her to his lap "—it gives you time alone with your handsome husband."

She leaned down and kissed his lips, then settled her head on his shoulder as he wrapped his arms around her and rocked her.

"Jesse?"

"Mmm?"

"You know the back room we were planning on finishing next summer?"

"Mmm," he murmured contentedly. "The one we were going to make a guest bedroom."

"Will you have time to finish it before then?"

"Probably. Why? Is your mother after you to visit?"

"Always."

Jesse chuckled and Amy closed her eyes, taking a moment to revel in the sound.

"You know Aunt Edna and Uncle Frank said they'd be glad to put her up until we get the house finished."

Amy straightened to look Jesse in the eyes. "We don't need the room for my mother." She smiled as the puzzlement on Jesse's face segued into understanding.

"Do you mean…?" He placed a large palm gently on her abdomen, where only a slight curve revealed the child inside. His comprehension changed into joy.

She covered his hand with her own and nodded. "During the storm."

He laughed and kissed his bride.

"If it's a girl, I'd like to call her Elizabeth."

He nodded. "And if it's a boy?"

Looking at each other, they blurted, "Damon." Still laughing softly, Amy snuggled against her husband. He embraced her, and together they sat for a long time, silently rocking as the day drew to an end. In the coming darkness, a bolt of lightning split the sky.

"Storm's coming," Jesse noted.

Amy nodded, settling into her husband's arms, listening to the beat of his heart, which matched her own. A clap of thunder followed the lightning. Soon rain would begin to fall. Jesse and Amy sat together content. They'd faced much bigger storms than this one. And won.